On Their Own
A Journey to Jamestown

Marie Stone

WHITE MANE KIDS
SHIPPENSBURG, PENNSYLVANIA

This book is a work of historical fiction. Names, characters, places, and incidents are products of the author's imagination and are based on actual events.

This White Mane Kids publication
was printed by
Beidel Printing House, Inc.
63 West Burd Street
Shippensburg, PA 17257-0708 USA

The acid-free paper used in this book meets the guidelines for permanence and durability of the Committee on Production Guidelines for Book Longevity of the Council on Library Resources.

For a complete list of available publications
please write
White Mane Kids
Division of White Mane Publishing Company, Inc.
P.O. Box 708
Shippensburg, PA 17257-0708 USA

ISBN-10: 1-57249-385-2
ISBN-13: 978-1-57249-385-8

Library of Congress Cataloging-in-Publication Data

Stone, Marie.
   On their own : a journey to Jamestown / Marie Stone.
      p. cm.
   Summary: Orphaned when a hurricane sinks their ship en route from London to the Jamestown Colony in 1627, twelve-year-old Amy, younger sister Sarah, and a third girl, Priscilla, are rescued by an Indian boy who guides them to the colony after a harrowing trip through the swamps.
   Includes bibliographical references.
   ISBN-13: 978-1-57249-385-8 (alk. paper)
   ISBN-10: 1-57249-385-2 (alk. paper)
   1. Jamestown (Va.)–History–17th century–Juvenile fiction. 2. Virginia–History–Colonial period. ca. 1600-1775–Juvenile fiction. [1. Orphans–Fiction. 2. Indians of North America–Virginia–Fiction. 3. Jamestown (Va.)–History–17th century–Fiction. 4. Virginia–History–Colonial period, ca. 1600-1775–Fiction.] I. Title.
   PZ7.S877940nn 2006
   [Fic]–dc22

                                                              2006042167

PRINTED IN THE UNITED STATES OF AMERICA

Contents

Part 1
The Journey

The Storm,
August 1627

All day twelve-year-old Amy Purdy sat curled up, listening to the savage storm. Was it trying to sink the ship? Every plank creaked. She prayed none of them would give way. Up topside, the wind howled like monsters fighting. If the ship broke in pieces, she knew she would die! The sailors had told Amy about hurricanes. *Is that what this is?* she wondered.

While the tempest raged, the sailors let no one on deck. Amy tried to sneak past the guard, but the sailors pushed her back. Cold seawater dribbled through a crack in the hatch onto the colonists crowded into the space between the deck and the hold. The smell of vomit made Amy gag. She held her breath, trying not to throw up like those other people had.

Amy had been sitting with these same colonists for all of the sixty-eight days the vessel had been sailing from England toward the New Land. She reached over and put another mark on the hull in her family's area to keep track. Every day she'd made a mark. In three more days it would be September. The *Mayflower* had crossed seven years before in sixty-five days. How come their ship, the *Hope,* was taking so long? Virginia was farther than Plymouth Colony, that was

3

true, but they'd been sailing more than two months and still she hadn't sighted land.

"We haven't even seen a bird," Amy complained to her father, who sat beside her trying to read by lantern light. "Everyone says you see birds first."

"You do, and we shall." Solomon Purdy looked up from his book. "Not in this wind, though. Birds can't fly in wind like this. They hide somewhere. Read. Like I am. You'll soon forget the storm."

Amy shook her head and glanced around at the other one hundred fourteen passengers. Sailcloth, used to divide the area into compartments for gentry folk like the Purdys and a large packed space beyond for commoners, had been torn down because of the storm. It had flapped each time the ship tossed and people tripped on it. Amy listened in when other passengers talked among themselves of how they hoped to have a fresh, successful life in the New Land.

She thought about Father telling her he wanted his family to enjoy life again. Since her mother had died of smallpox, almost a year ago now, Father talked of nothing else. "New beginning," he kept saying. "I need to get away from old memories. I shall treasure them here," he would say, tapping his head.

"It will be exciting to move to the New Land," Amy agreed.

"Not for me." Her sister, Sarah, shook her head. "I didn't want to leave England. It's scary out on the sea."

"You're frightened of everything. I wasn't always scared when I was seven," Amy told Sarah.

Right now, Sarah sat trembling and clutching Father, her eyes round with terror.

Amy wiped sweaty hair back from her forehead and pushed a sand-colored ringlet behind her shoulder. Her hair usually hung to her waist in soft waves. During the storm, in the humid ship, it curled into a bush.

The ship groaned as it took a sudden roll onto its beam-ends. Amy caught hold of Father so she wouldn't fall. She held her breath. The ship wouldn't go over, would it? She saw wet spots where water oozed between the planks. Across the crowded 'tween deck, a woman bandaged her husband's gashed arm. Amy had seen him fall against a nail. She saw blood on the boards where he'd hit. Blood dripped from the gash onto the hull right now, too.

Father settled Sarah in the Purdy family space and made his way across the heaving 'tween deck to help. He took hold of a sheet to stanch the bleeding, and when it stopped he tore the sheet into strips to bind the wound.

Amy forced her thoughts to the heap of books under her hammock. Should she read like Father had said? Throughout the voyage, he'd kept telling her she should be doing schoolwork. "A girl needs her studies," he had said more than once.

I've learned more already than any girl in the whole world, Amy thought. She knew plenty of girls her age who didn't have a tutor like she did. Priscilla Johnson, another passenger, didn't, and she was eleven. The three of them— Amy, Priscilla, and Sarah—were the only children on the ship. Amy knew the reason her father spent so much time teaching her and Sarah was because they didn't have any brothers for him to teach. She wondered what good memorizing the dates of all those kings and queens would do her in the New Land.

Right now, Priscilla sat with the other commoners and tried to sew. In nice weather Amy tutored her in reading. Priscilla had already learned to read almost as well as Sarah. Back home in England, Amy would never have met a girl from the working class.

Amy recalled how Priscilla had told her she lived in one small rented room in the east end of London. Amy had lived in a mansion outside of London with servants and stables. They'd sold the horses.

"The ship doesn't have room for them, but we shall buy more when we get to Virginia," Father had promised. He raised horses for hunting and racing, so she knew he'd keep his word.

He had also said, "You may talk to Priscilla while we're on the ship, since she's the only other girl, but when we get to Virginia, you associate with your own kind."

Amy'd wanted to defend her friend. She'd wanted to remind Father that Priscilla and her mother were tradesmen, not low class. It would be rude to say that to him, though.

Amy admired Priscilla. She could sew real clothes—petticoats and aprons. She didn't only embroider fancy pictures like Amy did. Priscilla had told Amy how pleased she was to be starting a new life. The two of them had sat on deck for hours, Priscilla's dark head resting against the main mast beside Amy's fair one. They'd told each other all about themselves.

"I'm traveling with my mother," Priscilla had said. "Mother worked all day in London and sometimes all night, too, so we could make this trip. She sewed for people who didn't want to do their own sewing."

Priscilla and her mother sewed now, even in the storm, so they'd have money once they got to Virginia. They sat together in the crowded end of the 'tween deck.

"How can you see?" Amy had asked, when she'd gone over to visit. "It's so dark I can't tell whether it's day or night, and you don't have your own lantern like Father and some of the others."

"'Tis light enough. When I'm at my mending, I forget about the wind and the rain," Priscilla had said.

Sitting by the mast one day, Priscilla said she liked to pretend she and her mother were giving up everything. But they didn't have much to give up. Priscilla said it had been two years since her father had died—from hard work, the surgeon had said. In Virginia they wanted women to be wives for men who had come over earlier. That's why most of the passengers on this voyage were women. "Perhaps I'll get a new father," said Priscilla.

Maybe she would. Amy knew lots of women didn't want to go to the New World. They didn't want to go to a place with bears and wolves and savage Indians who cut off a person's hair along with the flesh it grew out of.

They're so brave to come by themselves, Amy thought, *both of them so small and no father*. She'd asked her father why Priscilla was not much bigger than Sarah.

"Perhaps all she gets to eat is bread and potatoes, hardly ever any milk or meat," Father had said.

Someone opened the hatch. Amy's head jerked toward the welcome burst of clean air and salt spray that rushed down. The sudden gust blew out lanterns and candles, including Father's.

"'Tis a hurricane," the captain shouted. He said something else, too, but the wind whipped his words away. The hatch slammed shut, cutting off the brief gush of fresh air.

Women started tying clothing into bundles and muttering to each other. "The ship is sinking," one woman said.

"I wish they'd let me up top," Amy said to Father. "I could help. I'm not little like Sarah."

Father handed her a shawl. She put it around her shoulders. "It's safer below. Things topside are blowing overboard." Amy used the shawl to mop sweat from her brow.

The captain's grave face appeared at the hatchway again in another welcome burst of clean air. "Send those children on deck. We'll tie them to the mast. The masts will float better than anything else." He wiped rain from his face, his hair plastered flat. "Everyone find things that won't sink. Tie them together so you'll be able to save yourselves when the ship does go down. God help us all."

Father's hand gripped the back of Amy's gown. She trembled in spite of herself. "You don't need to hold me," Amy said. "I want to go where there's light. At least there's air a person can bear to breathe up top."

"Look after your sister," Father said. He guided her to a rope on deck and gave her a hug. She felt his kiss on her forehead and his tension right through her gown. Amy gripped the line strung from the bow to the stern so she wouldn't be blown overboard. Father turned to help Sarah. The wind howled even louder up here. Fingers of terror crept on the back of Amy's neck.

Sailors guided Sarah and Priscilla up the creaky ladder, all of them ghost white—even the seamen. A silver-haired sailor named MacPhee held Amy's shoulders and helped her along with his rough, weathered hands. "Be not frightened, lass," he shouted in her ear. But he sounded scared himself.

Every inch of Amy's skin prickled with dread. She could see nothing but loose things blowing every which way. She ducked as something flew past her ear so fast she had no idea what it was. Below, she had welcomed the chance to get up top with the clean air. Now, she wished she could go back down and cling to Father.

The whole world was gray—sky, water, ship, as gray as ashes. Gray spray masked everything. Waves, ship, and seamen all leaned with the wind. Amy leaned, too, and prayed nothing would knock her into the churning sea. She'd had to let loose of her cap and shawl so she could hold the rope. They immediately soared away. She sank to the deck and clung to the line.

What if she got flung into the water? Would she float? At that exact moment a cold wave crashed on deck and soaked her. But she held tight, spitting out salt water. The wave raced past and washed over the side. Now that she was wet, she was cold instead of hot. Her teeth chattered. She wished she still had the shawl.

Sarah crawled across the deck, shivering. She clutched the line beside Amy, her face gray-green like the sea. Sarah had pulled her cap over her forehead and her ears, almost covering her eyes, and it hadn't blown away yet. She looked funny that way.

Four strong hands, those of MacPhee and another seaman, gripped Amy's arms and pushed her toward the spot where she had sat with Priscilla and given her the reading lessons. While they read, they had settled on the lee side of the main mast to stay out of the wind. Now, with the wind blowing from all directions, Amy couldn't find a lee side to anything.

She gripped the mast and tried not to think about what could happen. The stub of the foremast stuck up from the deck beside her—broken off and washed away, she assumed. Sarah held on to the mast on her right, Priscilla the same on the left. Amy's cold fingers touched their equally icy ones when she reached around the mast. She squeezed them. Priscilla squeezed back. She had lost her cap, too. Her dark hair blew around her head in circles. Amy felt her hair blow, too, into her eyes, and her nose, and her mouth. She spit it out. Sarah had now stuffed her cap down the front of her gown. It made a bulge there and looked as funny as it had when pulled over her forehead.

MacPhee threw a rope around the girls. His fingers lashed it tight. "Don't be frightened," he shouted again. "Leave your arms outside the line and hold fast to the mast. Pull this end if you need to get loose. The rope will fall away. If the mast breaks off, you don't want to be bound to it underwater. You'd drown. Creep to the crosstrees and catch hold there. The mast will float, and the crosstrees will keep it from rolling."

Wisps of silver hair blew across the bald spot on MacPhee's head. Amy had seen him lots of times whistling while he worked. *I'll wager he doesn't feel like whistling right now,* she thought.

The drenching rain beat like hailstones. Sometimes the wind blew it right in Amy's face, choking her.

Finally the sailors lashed the last of the rope. The three girls could move nothing but their arms. The storm made way too much noise to bother trying to talk. Amy closed her eyes, but she couldn't close her ears. She hugged that mast so tightly she feared she'd make dents in it. She should think of something besides the storm. She made herself think about the letter she would write to her cousin Edmund back in England as soon as she got to Virginia. Edmund would never believe this savage storm.

"Grab that line, MacPhee," the captain shouted.

Wood cracked. "There goes the mizzenmast," someone yelled.

Amy's eyes flew open. The mizzen toppled overboard and hung suspended by rope until at last it broke free and tumbled into the waves. The sailors hadn't had a chance to tie anyone to it before it disappeared. *I hope our mast doesn't break*, Amy thought. *It's bigger and sturdier, perhaps it won't.*

She kept a secure grip on the end of the rope MacPhee said to pull if she needed to get loose. What if she was so terrified she forgot to pull it?

More pieces of the ship broke off and blew overboard. Seamen brought two women on deck and started tying them to whatever would float. Rich ladies, Amy knew. Priscilla's mother would be the last lady, and Father would be after all the women. Priscilla would have no one if her mother was lost. Had Father found something that would float if the ship broke up? Another crack. The main mast lurched. "Oh no." She gasped. "It's going!"

Sarah screamed.

MacPhee reached toward them.

With one enormous thundering crack, the mast crashed to the deck. All three of the girls screamed as it swayed over the side into the wild waves.

Drifting

Amy had to get farther up the mast. She remembered MacPhee's warning about being lashed to it underwater and pulled the end of the rope. Hanging onto other ropes, she squirmed and slid as fast as she could to the crosstrees. Sarah and Priscilla needed to hang on behind. Had she left them enough room? Every time the mast rolled and pitched in the churning sea, a wave splashed in Amy's face.

With her arms and legs wrapped around, Amy held on so tightly her fingers and knees got numb. The bit of wreckage heaved as if trying to fling her into the waves. She'd slide off for sure if she relaxed her grip. Every couple of seconds water sloshed over her, choking her and stinging her eyes.

Wind roared—the only noise she could hear. After a while the water didn't feel cold any more, because she was as chilled as it was. Behind her, she heard Sarah throw up. Was Priscilla all right? She didn't dare look. She was even afraid to look for the ship. Any movement could make her slip off.

Day turned to night. Amy lay and shivered on the mast. Still the rain stung like a million mosquitos. She couldn't sleep, even though she hadn't slept for what seemed like days. Amy thought of those enormous black fish with pointed fins that she had seen from the deck of the ship. Sharks, Father had called them. She hoped none were near. She'd never seen anything so mean looking. Right now she wouldn't be able to see one if it were right beside her. She could see nothing in the dark. The shark could reach over and chomp a bite out of her, and she'd never know it was anywhere near till she felt the teeth. Terror made her mind as numb as her body.

After what seemed an eternity, a faint glow showed in the sky. The waves stopped heaving. The rain stopped battering. The deafening sound of the wind abated. Amy looked over her shoulder. Sarah wasn't moving. She looked stiff and hadn't thrown up in a long while. "Are you all right, Sarah?" Amy shouted.

"Yes," Sarah answered through chattering teeth.

"How about Priscilla? All I can see of her is her head." Since the noisy storm had stopped its fury, Amy could hear the others talk.

"She's at my feet," Sarah yelled back. "I can feel her. I'm cold, Amy."

"Me, too. Are you all right, Priscilla?"

"Aye. I am," shouted Priscilla. "Can we paddle to shore? Which way is it?"

"I'm not letting go to paddle. And I have no idea where the shore is." Amy heard Sarah sob. "We should hang on and trust we end up somewhere safe."

"I guess so." Priscilla sounded unsure.

"Where's the ship?" Amy asked. She looked around as best she could at the empty sea. She still didn't want to wiggle. "I hope we go in at the same place it does."

Sarah raised her head to look, too. "It sank, Amy. I know it sank," Sarah cried. "I want Father."

Amy pretended she hadn't heard Sarah. She didn't want to consider the possibility that the ship, with all those people, especially her father, had gone to the bottom of the Atlantic.

"If it broke up, shouldn't we see people and pieces of wood in the water?" Priscilla asked.

"No people must mean it didn't." With that thought, Amy's tension relaxed. She'd find Father again.

At long last it stopped raining.

"Look!" Priscilla called. She pointed excitedly. "'Tis a shore line. I see it when we go up on the crest of a wave."

They went up again and Amy yelled, "Yes, I see it, too. A long white line on top of the water. Do you see it, Sarah?"

Sarah looked. "What if the ship did sink?"

"Don't keep saying that. Why would it go down if we didn't? It's probably washed up on that beach, same place we shall be."

"But I 'eard something else split apart as we went overboard," Priscilla said. "'Tis possible the ship broke into pieces. Remember what the captain said?"

"I don't see even a scrap of it in the water." But Amy knew Priscilla and Sarah could be right. They should see the ship if it had stayed afloat. She thought of her father with his kind eyes and smiling MacPhee, the sailor.

Their tiny bit of wreckage drifted and Amy watched the shore as if hypnotized.

Priscilla moaned. "I'm so thirsty. I must 'ave a drink. It 'as been almost two days since I 'ave 'ad one. My throat is going to close up."

"Don't drink the seawater," Amy cautioned. "It will make you sick. When we get to that shore, we'll find some."

"It's taking forever," said Sarah with a sob.

"I wonder how long it will take." Amy swallowed, trying to make her throat not so parched. But she didn't have any spit left to swallow.

They drifted all day and into the night. Darkness masked her view of the shoreline. It was like being set adrift all over again, like having the only security she had vanish in front of her eyes. What if that shore wasn't really there?

Amy peeked over her shoulder at both Priscilla and Sarah every few minutes to make sure they hadn't slipped off. Sarah lay clutching the mast and sobbing as if her whole life had been destroyed. Maybe it had.

Amy tried to think of something comforting to say, but she couldn't. She still felt those prickles on the back of her neck. Where could Father be? Again she hoped he'd found something to hold on to if he had been flung into the sea.

The night sky hung over them as black as a coal bin, the moon nothing but a sliver. Some of the clouds blew away, and now the inky sky had points of brightness where stars sparkled.

Amy clung to the wreckage and watched the sky instead of the water. She wondered if she could catch sight of that bright star her tutor had told her about. If she could find it, she'd know that direction was north.

She scanned the heavens. At last she saw it, directly in front of her. Polaris. So, north was straight ahead. The star appeared much closer to the horizon than when she had gone out in the garden with him that night in England. The ship had sailed a long way south. The two pointer stars sparkled beside it. They were in a sky picture called Ursa Major, her tutor had said. Amy never could see the pictures he pointed out, only the bright stars. *It is comforting to know we have the same sky up over us,* she thought. She smiled, first time in two whole days.

At last her eyes could stay open no longer. Even though scared and soaking wet, Amy slept soundly, plastered as securely to the mast as wallpaper is to a wall. In her dreams the debris she clung to stopped pitching about. The dreams changed from riding a jumping horse to serenely swinging.

Near morning, as she awakened, she heard something different in the sea sounds she'd been listening to for more than sixty days—waves on a beach.

We've come in to shore, she realized. Her eyes flew open. A bright sun shone on a long sweep of white sand stretching as far as she could see in two directions. It looked like it went on till it dropped off the ends of the earth. The clear blue water lapped at the shore with frilly white wavelets. The beach sloped up to a sand dune with grasses blowing in the wind—land smells again—sweet grass and trees.

"Wake up!" Amy called. "We've washed ashore."

Sarah jerked her head up.

Amy was wide awake now though a moment ago she'd been fast asleep. She blinked at the sun and focused on the shore as the wreckage grounded on the sandy bottom. Unwinding the ropes that held her to the mast, she rolled off and stood in the water. It came only to her knees. Priscilla and Sarah staggered to their feet beside her.

Land! After all those days at sea, what a relief to at last find land! But whose land? The land of the English, the Spanish, or the Savages?

On the Beach

Amy staggered to shore with the warm ripply waves licking at her ankles. The waves felt as pleasant as bathwater. She clutched at Priscilla to steady herself. "I've gotten used to the ship tossing beneath me," she said. "I can't walk." She sat in the sand and pulled off her shoes and stockings, dumping water out of the shoes and wiggling her toes. That felt good!

Standing up again, Amy squirmed out of her gown. The gown, heavy with water, dragged her down every step she took. She noticed two tears where it had been snagged on the mast. She tossed it up on a part of the beach far away from the sea to dry. Sarah put her rose gown with Amy's blue one and Priscilla laid down her plain gray frock. Amy and Sarah threw their petticoats up, too. Priscilla wore only her shift under her frock.

"This sand feels strange when I try to walk on it," Priscilla said, wrinkling her nose and carefully lifting one foot at a time. Cautiously, she stepped back down again. "I've walked barefoot on the dirt in London. T'wasn't like this at all. London dirt is soft and squishy after a rain. This is dry and scratchy."

Amy stood on the beach in her shift. "It's so silent. No houses. No people. Where can we be?" She squinted at the sun, which was climbing high in the sky.

"Nothing but sand, sky, and water," Priscilla said, chewing at her fingernails.

Reaching behind her, Amy bundled her long hair and wrung the seawater out of it. It streamed like a waterfall onto the beach. The hot sun touched her neck and arms. After rain for three days, heat felt good.

"We're lost," Sarah said. "The ship has gone down and we're all alone." She stuck her thumb in her mouth.

Amy ignored her. "I went to the seaside in England, with Mother before she got sick. It wasn't like this at all. The water felt a lot colder and the sand was nowhere near as white. Why aren't there big rocks or cliffs?"

Priscilla looked to each side and behind her. "I've never even been in a place like this. I boarded the ship from a dock in the river. In England I lived only in London, never any other place, not in my whole life." She chewed at her fingers again.

"I'm thirsty," said Sarah. "I'm going to look for a creek."

"Let's go straight up this hill," Amy said. "If we can walk, that is. Perhaps we'll see the ship if we get higher." Amy staggered up the rise. The loose sand felt toasty under her bare feet. Still the only sound was the occasional squawking of a seagull.

With her shift lifted above her knees, Sarah stumbled beside her sister, sinking to her ankles in the soft ground. Twice she fell flat on her face. Priscilla helped her to her feet. "Ooh. It is so difficult to walk," Sarah said, looking like she was about to cry again.

"It is," said Priscilla. "We shall have to learn all over."

"At least the land doesn't move like the water." Amy put a hand down and steadied herself. "It feels good to be on dry land, even if the walking is difficult."

She staggered past long waving wisps of seagrass growing in clumps partway up the dune.

Priscilla reached the top first. "I don't see the ship." She nibbled at her fingernails. "I 'ope it didn't sink."

"It did." Sarah glared at Amy and Priscilla with that determined expression she had when she felt she was right about something. "I know it did."

Amy tried to ignore her.

"Maybe the ship made it to Jamestown," Amy said. "Perhaps they'll send someone to search for us."

Priscilla nodded. "Aye. That must be it. I 'ope it is."

Now that she was on top of the dune, Amy saw even farther along the beach in both directions. No ship anywhere. Nothing but sand dunes. "It's odd we don't see any trees."

"Or people," said Priscilla. "I 'ave never before been anywhere that didn't 'ave people."

"What a big beach!" Sarah exclaimed.

Priscilla wandered along the top of the dune. "What's this sticking up above the sand? Come and look. Quick!"

Amy ran to join her, as fast as she could in the loose sand. Sarah followed, shuffling along behind.

Wooden beams poked out of the sand, timbers with decaying boards between—the hull of an old, old ship. One side stuck up like the ribs of a giant whale, the other lay buried beneath.

"That 'as been 'ere a long time," said Priscilla. "'Tis rotten."

"This is what happened to our ship. I know it." Sarah wiped her tears away. "Our ship is bones on the seashore somewhere."

"Saying that does no good, Sarah," Amy said. "And you're scaring me." She noticed a puddle of water trapped between two ribs of the ship's skeleton. Cautiously, she bent to taste it. Fresh—rainwater from the storm. She took a long drink and so did the others.

Wiping her mouth with the back of her hand, Amy said, "Now all we have to do is find something to eat."

Priscilla nodded. "I'm 'ungry, too."

Sarah sighed. "We haven't eaten for days."

"There must be fish in the ocean," said Amy. "Too bad we have no way to catch them."

Priscilla looked out over the sparkling waves, then back to the wreck. "I wonder what vessel this was. It looks ancient." She walked along beside it. "I'm looking for a name. If I can't read it, maybe you can, Amy." But she didn't find one.

"Perhaps it was a pirate ship," Sarah said.

At that suggestion, Amy raised both eyebrows and pushed back her hair. "It could have been. There isn't enough left to tell."

Her thoughts wandered back to the *Hope*. Could it already be rotting on a beach somewhere, like this one? What if Sarah were right? They'd be all alone in this strange New Land and they didn't know where it was. She'd think about something pleasant. She hoped she'd judged right and the ship had made it to Jamestown. And she hoped they'd find Jamestown close by.

Amy lowered her voice. "Look down the beach. Someone's here. See the funny marks in the sand? A pattern of some kind. Come on. Let's get closer."

"Be careful. It might be something that wants to eat us." Priscilla tiptoed behind.

Running down the dune sure was a lot easier than going up had been. Amy skidded on her bare feet with sand spraying out to each side. She slid so fast she went right into a jagged shell. Instantly she sat down and grabbed her wounded toe. Blood dribbled between her fingers.

"Oh no!" Priscilla exclaimed.

"I'll hold it a minute till the blood stops." Amy wiped her hands on her shift, leaving a red stain. After a minute, she said, "It's all right, now. I have to see those marks. Come on." She continued along the sandbar, reaching the imprints first and leaving a trail of blood where she had run.

The track went from the water, across the sand, to partway up the dune—slanted marks—as if someone had dug them in with an oar. Four rows of them, too, as far as Amy could tell, four rows carved in and overlapping each other. "I don't see anybody here to make them," she said in a whisper, as if someone might be hiding behind the sand dune listening.

"I'm scared," Sarah said. "Did a person make those marks, or an animal?"

"Doesn't look like either," Amy said. "No toe prints." She held her cut toe up off the sand and rested her heel on her other foot. Blood still dripped from the cut.

A large brown sea turtle lumbered out of the waves and pulled itself across the beach. "Look." Amy nudged Priscilla. "Look. A huge turtle came out of the sea, must be at least a yard across its back."

"It's making those marks we saw," Sarah said.

"Is that thing a turtle?" Priscilla frowned. "I've never seen a turtle before."

Another wave broke over the animal and washed away the track it had made. It swam a little and made twice as much headway as when it had walked. The water retreated, and the turtle waddled on up the sand, leaving more slanted marks behind.

A second wave and the turtle swam some more. It floated farther up the beach, almost in line with the girls. Amy kept her eyes on it, fascinated, until it got to where a clump of seagrass grew. The turtle turned around and started to dig a hole beneath its shell. Amy watched as it shuffled forward over the hole and began dropping round things into it.

"It's laying eggs!" she exclaimed. She counted eighty-two and stopped. The turtle pushed sand over her eggs and started the difficult trip back to the sea, crossing her own tracks as she moved on.

"So that's how the pattern was made. There must be a nest at the end of that other trail, too." Amy held her hair back and followed behind the turtle as the creature made its way to the water.

"Can you eat turtle eggs raw?" asked Priscilla. "I'm really, really 'ungry."

Sarah's mouth dropped open. "You wouldn't eat our turtle's eggs. Not after we watched her make that nest and lay them."

Priscilla walked over to where the first track ended. "No. This other one. Where we didn't see the mother."

The three girls dug in the sand with their hands till they had uncovered the nest of eggs. It took a while because sand slid into the hole as fast as they could dig it out. They each picked up an egg. It felt smooth but not hard like a chicken egg. It was like a piece of soft golden leather. Amy hit it against some driftwood, trying to smash it. Nothing happened.

Priscilla ran down the beach a few steps and came back with an oyster shell like the one Amy had slashed her toe on. "'Ere. Try slicing it with this."

Amy poked at the egg with the shell and a trickle of white and yellow oozed out. "Ugh. It's slimy. I can't eat that." She dropped the egg to the sand.

Sarah shook her head. "I can't either. I'd rather starve. Can't we cook them?"

"How? We can't make a fire. We have no flint or steel," Amy said.

Not one of the girls could bring herself to eat the gooey, warm eggs. They pushed sand over them and left them where they were.

"Can people live on only water?" Amy asked, sloshing her sliced toe in the sea to wash off more blood and sand. The salt water stung, but because it was cool, it made the toe feel better.

Amy limped back to the wreck for another drink, and when she'd finished, she turned to watch the sea again. "We must find a way to get to Jamestown." She set her mouth in a determined line. "There will be something to eat there."

"Aye. But where *is* Jamestown?" Priscilla looked around. "We don't even know which way to go. And can we walk there?"

"We have to try."

Sarah shook her head. "I'll never get back on a ship. Not ever. I'm glad I'm on land." She spoke with as much determination as Amy.

"But our families," Amy said. "Our father. Priscilla's mother. I'd get back on one. It's better than being alone."

Priscilla swallowed and tears trickled down her cheeks.

Sarah started to cry, too. She again stuck her thumb in her mouth.

Thinking she might never see her father again, or even any other people, started those prickles on Amy's neck once more. Tears welled in her eyes as she looked out at the shiny ocean.

"There's another turtle in the water," she said, wiping her nose on her hand and distracting everyone from their thoughts of how isolated they were.

The turtle drifted in a little with each wave. When its feet touched bottom, it slowly trudged across the sand like the other one had, making the same strange marks. Amy watched it, fascinated.

She noticed the sun now made long shadows on the grasses across the sandbar. The tide had come all the way in to the dry part of the beach and started to go back out again. "We spent a lot of time with those turtles," she said. "We'd better find our shoes and our gowns. I hope they haven't washed away."

Priscilla held up her shift and started to walk along the sand dune. "We 'aven't seen another living thing all day except those turtles."

"And some big white birds like you always see at the shore." Amy squinted at the sky.

Over the next hump of sand she spied the pile of clothes sitting in safety above the waves. Amy stuffed her stockings in her shoes and Priscilla put her frock back on. It had dried.

"My arms are hot and red," Amy said, holding them in front of her.

Sarah nodded. "Mine, too."

Priscilla looked at her own arms. They had turned as brown as toast.

"My gown is still damp," said Amy. "Sarah's too. I suppose it's because of the tucks, ruffles, and fancy stitching." Before she stepped into her petticoat and tied it at the waist, she tore off a strip of lace to bind her bleeding toe. Amy limped up the sand dune, carrying her gown and shoes. Sarah and Priscilla trudged along beside her.

Amy's long thick hair had finally dried. She pushed it out of her face for the hundredth time that day. "Will you braid my hair for me, Priscilla, please?" she said. "I want it out of my eyes."

Priscilla tried to braid Amy's hair in one long plait down her back. "'Tis tangled," she said. "I need a brush."

"We don't have one. It doesn't matter what it looks like. Weave the mats right in."

Priscilla braided the mats as best she could. "I must 'ave something to 'old it with," she said when she'd finished.

Amy pulled a ribbon out of her petticoat, and Priscilla wrapped it around to keep the hair from blowing in every direction.

"There," Priscilla said. "Now do me."

Amy braided Priscilla's hair, mats and all, and Priscilla did Sarah's at the same time. Since Priscilla didn't have a petticoat with a ribbon, Amy pulled another one out of hers.

"Where do we sleep tonight?" Sarah asked.

"Don't know," said Priscilla. "There isn't any wood 'ere to make a shelter, only that drowned ship we saw. What if it rains?"

"We could turn that wrecked ship over and it would be like a cave," Sarah suggested.

"But we'd be dumping out our water," Amy said. "Let's dig a hole. Up high so the tide won't get us. We'll be out of the wind that way."

"Nothing else we can do," said Priscilla. She shrugged.

Amy led as they hiked over the top of the dune and partway down the other side where the wind didn't blow quite so strong. She saw another stretch of water ahead of her.

"Oh no! We're on an island!" Amy said. "We have no food, and before noon tomorrow, we'll run out of water."

4   A Visitor

"We must find people," Amy said.

"Aye," said Priscilla. She looked at Amy and gulped.

Sarah wiped a tear from her eye. "What if we don't find any? What if we're the only people for miles?"

"Jamestown is somewhere near. We'll find Jamestown." But Amy didn't feel as sure of that as she sounded.

She and Priscilla scooped a nest for shelter in the sand, only stopping when the sand began to get damp. After going back to the wreck for another drink, Amy tumbled into the pit, exhausted, and before she could begin to worry about anything else, she fell asleep.

When rays of morning sun flickered across Amy's face, the first thing she noticed was her stomach rumbling with hunger. It had now been almost three days since she'd eaten. She spit out gobs of sand and wiped it from her eyes. If only she had a handkerchief, she could blow her nose.

She crawled out of the hole, not easy to do when her toe throbbed and felt like it was on fire. This morning the toe looked purple, and it had swollen to almost twice its normal size. She tore another strip of lace from her petticoat to rewrap it.

Pulling apart the petticoat, Amy thought of how her mother had made it for her before she got sick and died. She frowned when she saw how grimy the flounce had become. Taking the petticoat off, she placed it with Sarah's. Without the extra layer of cloth, she felt cooler and more comfortable.

She brushed sand from her bare arms and noticed that both of them were now salmon-pink from sunburn. She hadn't slept well and missed the swaying she'd felt on the ship for the past two months. Every one of her muscles ached. Even taking a few steps away from where she'd slept hurt. It had been weeks since she'd walked as much as she had yesterday. On the ship she'd had nothing to do but sit, read, and talk.

But she needed to see if the ship had turned up, so she gritted her teeth, hiked to the top of the dune, and scanned the ocean. Tiny waves ran up on the beach without making a sound. No ship floated on them.

Amy wiggled her toes in the sand, all except for that gashed one, and thought about a morning meal. What could she eat? Maybe she should go back to those turtle nests. She still didn't want to eat any slimy eggs, though. Priscilla might have an idea.

She wandered along the dune wishing she would come around a corner and suddenly see the *Hope*. But she didn't find any corners. If the ship was out there, she'd have seen it by now.

She turned and walked to the shore she'd noticed yesterday on the opposite side of the sand dune. When she reached it, she bent over and took a handful of water to taste. Yuck, salt. So this was part of the ocean. That confirmed they had come in on an island. How could she get to any people, a town or a village, when she was on an island? She had yet to see even one person. She held her shift up in a bunch in front of her and waded out in the lukewarm water.

At first it stung her toe, but then felt so nice on the rest of her sunburned legs she soon forgot that. Reaching down, she splashed cool water on her burnt arms and face, too.

Sarah's voice drifted across the beach. "She can't have gone far. I wonder why she took off her petticoat. Amy!"

Amy waved her arms and shouted, "Here I am!"

Priscilla's head appeared from behind a clump of weeds, followed by Sarah's. "Oh—you're bathing!"

"Wading," Amy called. "Up to my knees is all. I'm washing off my cut toe." She kicked away at the wavelets. "It's warm. Feels good."

"You come out of there and put your clothes back on," Sarah yelled.

Amy bent to splash a handful of water on Sarah, but it didn't get that far. "There's no one here to see me. It's heavenly after all that time with nothing but a pot of water to wash in. Get your feet wet, too."

"I'm going to," Priscilla said. She took off her frock, carefully folded it, and placed it on the dry part of the sand. Rolling her shift to the top of her legs like Amy had hers, she tested the water with her toe and waded in.

With a look of disapproval, Sarah sat on the sand and rubbed her sunburn.

Amy and Priscilla splashed and chased each other in the ripples. "Aren't you hot, Sarah?" Amy called.

"Yes, but I'm not taking my clothes off. You're sinful, Amy. It's sinful to let people look at your skin."

"What people?" Amy glared at her sister.

She and Priscilla splashed in the sea until fatigue took over. It didn't take long.

"I'm not going to wear my frock," said Priscilla. "'Tis easier to walk in this sand without it. Go back and get yours. We'll wait for you before we try to find something to eat."

Sarah had put her gown back on while the other girls waded in the water. She frowned at them. But Amy didn't care one speck what Sarah thought.

She retrieved her gown and said, "I guess we'll have to get those turtle eggs." She wrinkled her nose like she'd tasted something nasty. "I don't know if I can eat them raw."

"We 'ave to," Priscilla said. She made a face like Amy. "There's nothing else. We'll starve if we don't. I'm so 'ungry I could eat almost anything."

Sarah walked along the sandbar that the outgoing tide had formed. "Look at these little holes," she called. "I think they're clams. Remember how we saw people digging clams in England? Remember, Amy? When we were staying in our home at the shore?"

"I'd eat clams. I've had them before." Amy hobbled to look at what her sister had found.

Sarah continued. "Find a hole and dig fast." She pointed at the sand.

"I can't imagine 'aving two different 'ouses," Priscilla said, shaking her head. "I didn't even live in a 'ole 'ouse, only a single room. I've never dug for clams before, either."

"Neither have I," said Amy. "But I've seen others do it. It looked easy. Watch me."

Priscilla poked her toe into one of the holes. The clam buried there squirted up at her, making her squeal and jump back. "I know what clams are, though. Mother bought them, and oysters, too, from the fish seller on the streets of London."

Amy led the other girls out on the sandbar. Quite a bit of it showed now. She got down on her knees and demonstrated how to dig with her hands until she had uncovered a fat white clam shell.

Priscilla joined her and started digging as well. "'Tis easy."

"Do we have to eat them raw?" Sarah asked. She sat and watched the others.

"How could we make a fire?" Amy asked. She grimaced. "Dig, Sarah."

Sarah continued to watch while Amy and Priscilla did the work. Soon a pile of four dozen or so clams sat on the sand beside them.

"Give me your cap to put them in, Sarah," Amy ordered.

"No," said Sarah. "I don't want to be naked like you are. Remember, Mother said never to go outside without your cap?"

"Who's here to see? Anyway, it isn't naked because you don't have your cap on. Being naked is having no clothes at all. So I'm not naked either. I've got my shift on." Amy turned her back on her sister.

Sarah sat with a pout.

"I'll go back and get my petticoat to wrap them in." Amy limped to where the clothes had been left.

While returning, she noticed a log with a lump on it floating on the water off in the distance. It hadn't been there before. The lump looked like a person, and the log was moving much too fast to be drifting.

Is it a little boat? Amy wondered. "Look!" she yelled to Sarah and Priscilla. "Out on the sea!"

The piece of driftwood moved closer and closer to shore, directly toward the three girls. Holding hands, Priscilla and Sarah stepped over to Amy.

"'Tis coming here," said Priscilla, sounding alarmed. "Should we 'ide?"

"Yes. He might be Spanish. Up in the grass. Hurry." Amy pointed up the dune.

Sarah dropped Priscilla's hand and bolted to safety.

Amy flung her petticoat down on the sandbar, filled it with the clams they had dug, and hurried after Sarah into hiding.

Priscilla picked up her frock and Amy's gown as she passed them. With Priscilla and Sarah, Amy hid herself behind a hill of sand where clumps of weed grew.

Her heart pounded like it was trying to escape her chest. She hoped the person on the log couldn't hear it. If it were a Spaniard, she'd not say a word so he couldn't tell she was English.

"He'll see the 'oles we've dug," whispered Priscilla.

"Perhaps he'll land someplace else," Amy whispered back. "Then he won't know we're here."

All Sarah said was, "I'm scared." She stuck her thumb in her mouth again and wiggled farther and farther into the sand. All of the girls kept their eyes on the person floating in on the piece of driftwood.

As the log got closer, Amy saw the paddler had dark brown skin, as if he had been in the sun a lot. His black hair had been shaved off at the sides. It stood in a ridge on top of his head and looked like a hedgerow in England. Light-colored things were stuck in the hair. *I hope they aren't the bones of people he's killed*, Amy thought.

"He must be an Indian," she whispered to Priscilla. "I've heard of Indians. They're the people who lived here before we came."

"At least 'e isn't Spanish," Priscilla whispered back, "or a pirate."

Sarah took her thumb out of her mouth. "Indians are savages," she said. "He'll kill us and eat us."

Priscilla glared at her. "All 'e's got on is a ripped shirt."

"You don't have much more on," said Amy.

"He's seen our holes in the beach," Sarah whispered. "He's coming in where we dug the clams. I don't like the way he doesn't have hardly any clothes."

"Aye. I don't either," said Priscilla.

"Stop talking. We don't want him to hear us," Amy said through her teeth, thinking of the stories she'd heard of Indians killing white people. Sarah had good reasons to be scared. Sweat ran down Amy's back. She felt as terrified now as she had in the storm.

She held her breath and watched as the savage ran his craft up on the sand. It was a slice of a big tree. The middle had been hollowed out so there was a place to put things and to sit. He leapt out, pulling his log boat on shore behind him.

Taking a long skinny pointed thing with him from the canoe, he walked over to the holes dug in the beach. Could that long thing be a spear? The Indian looked up and down the shore, then followed the girls' footprints across the wet sand. Hiding had done no good.

"Oh, no. He's coming straight for us." Sarah put her hands in front of her face, as if she thought he wouldn't be able to see her that way.

Amy huddled in the sand hardly daring to breathe, but she kept her eyes open and fixed on the Indian. Would he kill them? Would he cut their hair off? Did savages eat English people like that sailor on the *Hope* had said?

The Indian

The stranger made his way to the top of the sand dune and gaped at the girls huddled behind the clump of grass. "English," he said. And he laughed.

"He thinks we're comical." Amy didn't take her eyes off him.

Priscilla sighed with relief when he laughed.

Sarah kept her eyes closed tight and her hands in front of them.

Amy stood behind the grass. She came up almost to his nose. He had a smooth face, no beard like her father, so he must be young. Grownups always had whiskers. *Maybe he's not much older than I am*, she thought. *Fifteen perhaps?* His eyes looked like two blots of black ink. Everyone in her family, and Priscilla and her mother, too, had blue eyes.

She got a closer look at the clothing he wore. A long sleeveless shirt, made out of animal skins, hung almost to his knees. It covered only one of his broad shoulders. Or the garment might have been a short skirt with one strap part. Amy didn't know what to call it. He wore nothing on his feet. Black circles with large dots in the middle, looking like targets, had been painted on his skin at the ends of each shoulder. The light-colored things she'd noticed before, stuck in his ridge of hair, turned out to be feathers and shells, not bones.

"Come on, Sarah, open your eyes and look at him." Amy nudged her sister. "He won't hurt you—I hope."

Sarah kept her hands in front of her face and lay in the sand shivering.

Priscilla stood and wrapped her arms around herself, trying to cover her bare skin and her shift. "We don't even 'ave our frocks on," she whispered.

Amy shrugged. "Too late to do anything about that now."

The petticoat with the clams inside started to slip from her grip. She tried to catch it, but the clams dropped to the sand.

"Ah!" the Indian said. He started to pick them up.

"Those are ours," said Amy. "Give them back." But she didn't want to protest too much. What would he do?

Taking Amy's petticoat from her, he wrapped the clams again and made a motion for the girls to follow. He headed to his canoe. "Eat," he said.

"He said an English word," said Priscilla.

Amy raised both eyebrows.

Sarah had her eyes open now, round and wide. She trembled and stared, her mouth gaping, as she peeked out from behind her sister.

Amy took Sarah's hand and pulled her to her feet. Sarah held Priscilla's on the other side. Hesitantly the three of them followed the Indian. He looked back every few steps as if he wanted to make sure they came behind.

"What do you suppose 'e'll do?" Priscilla whispered.

"I have no idea, but he's got our clams, so I'm going with him." Amy didn't know whether to be frightened or not. She hoped, since he smiled, it meant he didn't plan to kill them.

The Indian put the clams on the sandbar then went to his canoe where he got some sticks. He gathered dry grass and started rubbing the sticks together over it, glancing up at Amy every once in a while.

Soon a puff of smoke drifted from the grass. Quickly he fed more grass, and tiny pieces of wood, until he had a flame.

"He's made a fire!" Amy exclaimed. "What a way to do it! Why doesn't he use a flint? Do you think he'll cook our clams?"

"He won't eat them all and not give us any, will he?" Sarah whispered. She had come out into the open now.

Priscilla shook her head. She didn't look frightened any more. "He acts nice. Let's collect wood and 'elp." Amy joined Priscilla to search for bits of driftwood.

Sarah sat with her eyes fixed on the Indian, watching his every move. She still looked ready to run.

When he had a fire blazing, he tossed the clams into the coals, then sat back and grinned again. Amy's mouth watered as the clams she'd worked so hard to dig up slowly opened. When they were finally ready, he pinched them between two sticks, one by one, and passed them to the girls.

"Eat," he said again.

"Thank you," Amy said, protecting her fingers with the hem of her shift as she took the hot clam. The first one she passed on to Sarah. She didn't think her sister would take one directly from the Indian. The second she kept for herself, saying "Thank you," again.

"T'ank oo," the Indian repeated.

Priscilla giggled.

Amy ate clam after clam until all of them were gone. Sarah did, too, and Priscilla. Nobody talked. The girls chewed and swallowed, chewed and swallowed. At last Amy wiped her hands on her shift and said, "This is as good a meal as the best roast beef I've ever eaten."

"'Tis because you've never been this 'ungry before." Priscilla swallowed her last clam and licked her fingers. "I've been 'ungry lots of times."

With Sarah and Priscilla sticking close by, Amy went back to the wreck to drink the last of the rainwater. "We need to find another way to get water," she said. "People can't live without it. We'll die in a day or two if we don't find some."

"Aye, we will," Priscilla agreed, nodding.

Sarah stuck her thumb in her mouth.

When they had returned to the canoe, Amy suggested, "We should tell him our names. Watch me." She pointed to herself with both thumbs. "I'm Amy," she said. "Amy."

Priscilla got the idea. She pointed to herself. "Priscilla."

Then Sarah copied the older girls. "Sarah." She pointed to herself with her thumbs like Amy had.

Amy went over it again, "Amy." She pointed to herself. She put her hand on her sister's shoulder, "Sarah," then Priscilla's, "Priscilla."

The Indian seemed to catch on. He put his hand on Amy's shoulder. "Amy," he said. Then on Priscilla's, "Priscilla." Only he left off the "Pr" and said "'Iscilla." When he tried to touch

Sarah, she jumped away and hid behind Amy again. After he had practiced the girls' names, he pointed to himself with both hands and said something that sounded like Cokwaiunkwas. The girls couldn't begin to copy it.

"We're unable to say your name," Priscilla said.

"It sounds like a whole sentence," said Sarah, coming out from behind her sister.

"We'll make up a new name for you." Amy looked at the others. "Any ideas?"

"I've always liked Thomas," Sarah said.

Amy shook her head. "No good. It's an English name. We need something that goes with where we are."

"But we don't know where we are," Sarah pointed out.

"Sometimes in England people are named after places," Priscilla suggested. "We are going to Virginia. Let's call him Virginia."

"The colony is named after a lady," Sarah said.

"It is still the name of the place. And is that truly where we are? We might be miles away." Amy glanced at him again.

"Aye, but we do know we're in the New Land."

"You want to call him New Land? That isn't a name. We'll call him Virginia. I like that idea. It shows we hope that's where we are." Amy looked at the others for approval.

"Or it shows that's where we want to get to," Priscilla said. Amy wondered, if not Virginia, what else could this place be?

"We're going to call you Virginia," she said to the Indian. She pointed to him. Then she put her hands on his shoulders and again said, "Virginia."

He laughed. "Virginia," he repeated, pointing to himself.

Virginia took two steps toward his canoe and said, "Go. English." He made a motion for them to follow.

"'E wants us to go with 'im somewhere," Priscilla said, her fingertips finding her mouth again.

"Maybe he knows more people like us and he'll take us to them," said Amy. "He keeps saying 'English', and he has used some English words. He must be aware of other colonists."

"Should we go?" Priscilla asked.

Sarah hung back. "Not me. I'm scared. What if he goes somewhere where lots of savages are and they're mean? What if they kill us?"

"He cooked our clams," Amy pointed out. "And we can't stay here. If we stay here we'll die of starvation before anyone ever finds us."

Sarah sat on the sand, folded her arms, and set her jaw in a straight line. "I'm not going."

"But Father doesn't know where we are. He can't tell searchers where to look. If we get to other people, we can send him a message. We must go. Do you want to stay here and die?"

Priscilla pushed her braided hair back over her shoulder. With a frown she said, "'alf of me wants to go. 'Alf of me wants to run." She seemed to be trying to talk herself into it. "I'm so worried about my mother. Perhaps our ship did make it to Jamestown, like you said. Perhaps she's there waiting for me. Perhaps that's where he'll take us."

Sarah sniffed and clutched her gown around her. "Not me."

Amy tried to get a hold on her sister's wrist. But Sarah kept her arms folded and her hands tucked under her arms.

"Come on, Sarah," Priscilla pleaded. "We 'ave to trust him. There's nothing else we can do. 'E's friendly. 'E cooked the clams. Other Indians will be nice, too."

Sarah didn't move.

Virginia turned on his way to the water. "Come," he said. He threw sand on what was left of the fire as he passed it.

Amy took advantage of her sister watching Virginia to grab Sarah's elbow. She yanked Sarah to her feet, wrapped her arms around her, and held both of Sarah's arms tight against her sides. Priscilla pushed from behind, and the two of them dragged her to the canoe.

Sarah screamed and tried to wriggle away, but could do nothing with the two older girls holding her. "I don't want to go. I don't want to." She tried to bite her sister.

Virginia watched them with raised eyebrows.

"Get our clothes, Priscilla." Amy panted from the exertion, but still held tight to Sarah.

Priscilla let Sarah go and got the gowns and shoes.

Amy wrapped her arms tighter around Sarah and looked the boat over. "It's small," she said. "There aren't any seats, only some long skinny sticks and one or two roundish bowl-looking things made out of wood lying in the bottom." Amy had no idea what any of the objects were. She also saw a bow and some short sticks that must have been arrows.

Priscilla nudged Amy and pointed in the canoe. "Look— 'tis a real knife like I've seen before in England! Proves 'e knows English people. 'E 'ad to get it from someone."

"How can you tell it's English? Couldn't it be Spanish?" Amy swallowed and frowned. "I hope he didn't kill an Englishman to get it."

The dugout puzzled her. She wasn't sure what to do. "Do we sit in the bottom since there aren't any seats?"

Priscilla put the clothes in. Then she put her hand on the canoe as if to test the balance. It rocked a bit.

Virginia grasped the other side and steadied it.

Amy lifted Sarah into the canoe and stepped in after her. Both of them sat toward the middle and Priscilla got in the front, immediately starting to chew on another nail.

Sarah shook, her teeth chattering. "There's no room. Do you think it will sink like the *Hope* did?"

"It won't." Amy slid back as far as she could and still leave a seat for Virginia. Not an inch of space remained. She held tight to her sister's wrist in case Sarah decided to jump out.

This is the right thing to do, Amy told herself, as icy fingers of doubt crawled up and down her spine.

6

English

Virginia put his pointed stick and his fire-starting sticks in with the other things. The canoe floated as he pushed it out into the water. He stepped in behind Amy, taking up the last inch of space. A mouse would have found it crowded. The canoe skimmed over the water when he pushed against the bottom of the bay with one of the long skinny poles.

As soon as they'd got far enough from shore that Sarah couldn't walk back, Amy let go of her. Sarah then gripped both sides of the dugout so tightly her knuckles turned white.

"I guess I didn't want to stay on that beach by myself anyway," Sarah muttered.

Amy looked ahead to where she could see real trees in the distance. "Good," she said, "something besides sand." Now, with the hot sun beating on skin that had always been covered by hair, the back of her neck felt like it had burst into flame. She scooped up handfuls of water to splash on her nape, trying to cool the burning skin. It did no good.

"This water is a lot cleaner than the Thames," Priscilla remarked, splashing water on her arms like Amy.

"I suppose people here don't throw their garbage into it." Then Amy remembered she hadn't yet seen any people to throw garbage. She wiggled her sore toe and prayed they were headed for wherever Virginia had learned those English words.

Birds circled overhead, birds Amy had never seen before and others she had been looking at in England her whole life, most of them big and white. She kept a good lookout for more turtles but didn't see any. Maybe Virginia would know how to cook their eggs.

He paddled while the sun traveled overhead, then started its descent in the west. Amy could tell by the path of the sun that they were headed north.

At last Virginia brought the canoe to shore on a small, flat, sandy island, different from the place they had been for two days. This place not only had white sand with the occasional clump of grass, but also real trees, some of them quite large. No brush grew beneath the trees, as if someone had cleared it away. That had to mean people! Amy kept her fingers crossed.

"English," he said again. But no people of any kind could be seen.

"Why does he keep saying 'English' when no one is around?" Amy whispered.

Priscilla shook her head and tore at her fingernails with her teeth.

Amy got out, followed by Priscilla and Sarah. Cautiously, and walking on her heel so she wouldn't scrape her cut toe, she took a wary step onto the island.

Virginia leaped to shore behind them. He pulled the canoe up on the sand and stood beside it. "English," he said again, and pointed up into the trees. He stayed by the canoe while the girls headed inland.

Only Sarah had her shoes back on. The other girls still walked barefoot. Amy watched for animals or people. Nothing moved. Would they meet savages? Would the savages jump out at them and kill them?

"It's so silent," she whispered.

"Aye. Not even an animal sound," Priscilla whispered back. She frowned and moved closer to Amy.

"But it does look like people have been here," Amy said, forgetting to whisper. She quickened her step and continued through the trees. "Doesn't this walkway look like it has been cut?" She pointed to a stump with ax marks. "A path can't make itself."

"An animal could make a trail," Sarah said.

"Not with an ax," said Amy. She passed the trees and came to a clearing with stones set on the ground in house-sized rectangles—lots of rectangles. "They've been put there on purpose," she said, "like a child would do with toy blocks."

Priscilla chewed another nail. "Do you think 'ouses used to be built on those piles of rock?" she asked, looking in all directions. "What could have 'appened to them?"

"Perhaps the houses blew away," Amy suggested, "in a storm like the one we had on our ship."

Priscilla nodded, and her frown relaxed.

Amy felt an icy shiver scoot down her spine. People had built something here. That was a certainty. Rocks didn't lie in rectangles by accident. Did Indians build houses that way? But if people had tried to make houses, what had happened to the people? Had someone killed them? If so, where were the bodies? Would someone come now and kill her and Priscilla and Sarah?

Priscilla whispered, "I don't like it. You don't suppose this is all there is of Jamestown, do you?"

"Can't be. Jamestown is a whole village. Father said. It has lots of houses and shops and fields," said Sarah.

"And people. Father said before we left England that more than two thousand people lived in Jamestown." Now Amy frowned. "There would have to be places for ships to tie up, too."

In a voice so low Amy hardly heard it, Priscilla said, "This is a ghost village."

"I'm scared," said Sarah. She bolted back to the canoe.

Amy and Priscilla continued to wander through the deserted community, Priscilla with her teeth chattering. Beyond the ruined houses, Amy found dry plants growing up higher than her knees and set out in rows. "Someone has tried to grow crops here."

"'Twas many years ago. Big weeds are growing in with the rows." Priscilla reached for Amy's hand but missed.

Beside the lines of parched plants, she found mounds of dirt making a high barrier around a large circular dent in the ground. More than fifty people could have gotten inside the hollow. She climbed over the wall of dirt. It came up past her head. Walking down into the low spot in the middle, she said, "It's kind of like a castle. I made things like this in the sand when I was at the shore in England, then I played I was a knight."

Priscilla wandered off beyond the castle. "Look at this tree," she called. "It's got letters on it. Come and look, Amy. You can read. What does it say?"

Amy ran over. "C-R-O-A-T-O-A-N," Amy spelled out. She raised an eyebrow. "It's a word, but no word I've ever seen before. I don't know what it means."

Priscilla grabbed for Amy's hand again and tugged. "Come on. Come on. Let's go. This place is frightening. There's nothing 'ere but spirits. We don't want to meet any of those."

"I hope Virginia doesn't think this is where we want to get to and leave us here." Again Amy spoke in a whisper.

Amy and Priscilla ran, hand in hand, back to the shore, Amy running lopsided because of keeping her toe up. Virginia stood by the dugout. Sarah sat in it with her hands in her lap, chewing on her lip, and looking like she was about to break out in tears.

"Let's go, Amy. Let's go." Sarah sat in the center, as if she thought that was the safest spot. "Hurry!" she urged.

Amy jumped into the canoe behind her sister as fast as she could without overturning it. Priscilla got in in front of Sarah.

"Go," Amy ordered. "Hurry. Go." She felt safer in the boat with Virginia, relieved that she was no longer in that spooky village.

Virginia pushed the canoe into the water, then used his paddle. The canoe moved silently away from shore. "Hurry," he said, as if practicing the word. "Hurry. Go."

As the dugout moved far from shore, the mysterious island disappeared behind them. Sarah quivered with fear as she watched it fade away.

Amy glanced around. The shore ahead was clearer now. No evidence of people. No buildings. No boats. No smoke from fires. There was a thick forest bordered by a strip of sparkling white sand.

"It's prettier here than it is in a city," Amy said. "If we weren't lost I would like it." She dipped up a handful of seawater to cool her face and neck.

"Aye," agreed Priscilla, splashing water like Amy, "I would too."

"Except for the ocean we crossed in the *Hope*, I've never been on this much water before," Amy said. She knew it couldn't be the wide open ocean, with nothing between her and England, because she'd spent two days on that beach with the turtles. That was between. It must be some kind of inlet or bay, but the biggest one she'd ever seen. "What will we find on the other side?" she asked. "Jamestown? An Indian village? Virginia keeps saying 'English'."

No one answered.

The far shore, when they finally got close enough to see it, had enormous trees growing close to the water's edge. Not even one tree was as skinny as the ones in the deserted colony. These trees had sturdy trunks, wide spreading branches, and were so huge she felt sure they'd been growing there for years and years.

Something gray, filmy, and spidery hung from the boughs. Amy had never before seen anything like that gray stuff. It looked like cobwebs, but hung down a full foot and a half and was made of thick threads instead of delicate ones. Did spiders build webs in trees? If they did, the spiders that lived in this place must be the size of alley cats. She shivered at the thought.

Virginia paddled along the shore. Amy peered anxiously into the forest, hoping to glimpse something, anything, that would mean people. She saw nothing. She pointed at the forest and asked, "English?"

"Eat," he said.

Amy wondered what strange thing they would have now.

Virginia put down his paddle, picked up a sharp-pointed stick, and watched the water.

"Sit still," Amy cautioned, sitting like a statue. "If we move, I fear the boat will tip."

After a minute or two, Virginia thrust his long stick into the water. When he pulled it out, a fish wiggled on the end.

"It's a spear!" Sarah exclaimed. "I wondered what he was doing."

"What a way to catch fish," Amy said. "I thought people always used a net."

Virginia thrust his spear into the bay several more times. Soon four fish flip-flopped in the bottom of the dugout, one for each of them.

"*Nammais*," Virginia said as he put the fish down.

"*Nammais*," Amy repeated. "Must mean fish," she said to Priscilla, who nodded.

After putting his spear down, Virginia paddled for shore. The girls hopped out, then Amy and Priscilla helped pull the canoe onto the sand.

Holding hands, Amy, Sarah, and Priscilla walked warily toward the woods. Amy didn't see any huge spiders, only a long snake that slid off into the brush.

Sarah instantly screamed and jumped behind Amy.

Priscilla shuddered. "Ugh. I 'ate things that squirm. They make me feel creepy."

Amy pulled some of the gray stuff down so she could get a closer look. It had soft, thick strands woven together like the chain mail suit of armor she'd seen once in a castle. "We still haven't seen spiders," she said. "So it must have been made some other way."

"Good," said Priscilla. "I don't want to come across giant spiders that 'ang in the trees waiting to drop on my 'ead when I don't expect 'em to."

Virginia got his fire-starting sticks from the canoe, and soon a campfire crackled away on the beach.

"Help me collect wood," Amy said. But Priscilla had already started.

"Try to get small, dry pieces," said Priscilla.

By the time the sun had gone down in a blaze of orange and red, the travelers had full bellies and had made themselves nests in the warm sand.

Amy tried to snuggle into the sand, but that was impossible. The ground was as hard as rock and rubbed on her sunburn. She watched the embers fade. On the other side of the fire, Virginia snored softly.

"I wonder where he'll take us tomorrow," Amy whispered. Shivers of dread crept over her. Would it be a place with bad Indians? She looked at Priscilla and Sarah lying wide awake beside her and trembled at the thought. "We go where he says. We have no choice in that."

7 Paddling Along

Next morning Amy and Priscilla walked out on a sandbar and dug clams for their morning meal. As before, Amy put them in her petticoat to carry back to the campsite. "If you're going to follow me every place I go, Sarah, at least help scoop up the clams," Amy said, glowering at her sister.

Sarah shook her head and poked her toe in a clam's hole.

Priscilla rolled her eyes.

Back in camp, Amy tossed the clams into the fire Virginia tended and sat down to look at her toe. She grimaced when she saw what a dark crimson mess it was. She figured it was twice the size it had been two days ago. White pus oozed out of the cut now, too.

Virginia looked at the toe, then headed into the forest. He returned to hand her long, pointed leaves. "*Messetts*," he said and pointed to her toe.

"What does 'e want you to do?" Priscilla chewed on that nail again. "What do you suppose *messetts* means?"

Amy shrugged.

He said something else Amy didn't grasp, then made a motion as if putting something on his foot.

She placed the leaves against her toe. "This?" she asked.

He nodded. "Ah."

She wrapped the lace back around, tying the leaves against her toe. "Maybe *messetts* means foot." She shrugged. "If nothing else, the toe doesn't hurt so much with the leaves cushioning it."

After everyone had eaten, Priscilla and Amy bundled up the leftover clams and loaded them into the dugout. Sarah watched.

"Help, Sarah," Amy ordered. "I'm getting tired of you sitting around watching everyone else work."

Sarah shook her head. "Ladies don't load canoes."

Amy glared at her. "You've got skin hanging off your nose. It looks ugly."

She spotted a yellow feather lying on the sand and stuck it in her hair. She grinned at Virginia. Then she, Priscilla, and Virginia pushed the dugout into the water.

Sarah sat in the back this time, next to Virginia. "I can tell he's nice," she said, "for a heathen. Someone who cooks for us can't be a murderer."

Amy nodded. "Maybe all those stories you hear about savage Indians are just that, stories."

"Fairy tales," said Priscilla.

As Virginia paddled along an arm of the sea, a black bear peeked out between the trees. Amy threw her arms up in front of her face and Sarah screamed.

When they'd passed the bear, Amy picked up one of the skinny things stored in the bottom, another paddle. Looking up at Virginia with a questioning look, she made paddling motions to ask if she could help. He nodded, so she guessed she could.

As the canoe glided along, Amy looked for houses or fires. She saw only enormous trees, their trunks and branches covered with bright green moss. Spreading ferns sprouted beneath the trees. "Nothing is the same as England," she remarked. A prickle of fear scooted down her spine. What was in that forest? More bears? Bad Indians? Something else? It was too dark to see anything.

"'Tis not knowing," said Priscilla. "Not knowing where we are. Not knowing where we're going. Not knowing if there will be anything to eat for supper. Not knowing why that word was on the tree. That's the bad part."

Amy nodded and gulped.

Rustlings in the underbrush told her animals hid there, maybe more bears. Lots of birds flew through the trees. Most of them had dark feathers, not white like the ones on the shore. Some were as large as the shore birds or even larger. Every once in a while a fish, or something else, swam beneath the dugout.

Virginia turned the canoe into a river. It was even darker now, because branches hung far over the water. Amy reached up to pluck a leaf from where she sat. Sarah screamed again when another fat bear came to the edge and put his paw in to scoop out a fish.

"There's nothing to screech about. He can't get us out here," Amy said. "At least I hope he can't."

"'E only wants the fish." Priscilla swatted at an enormous black insect buzzing in her face.

Sarah stuck her thumb in her mouth and scowled.

The paddling continued for a whole week. Amy's arms and shoulders stopped aching so much and the work got easier every day. More animals came to drink. A deer came, and several smaller critters with ringed tails. "Are they monkeys?" Sarah asked, without screaming, when the first ringed-tailed animal appeared.

Virginia seemed to realize what Sarah was talking about. "'Coons," he said. "Raccoons."

"'Coons," all the girls repeated. "Raccoons."

Priscilla shivered when a black eel swam beneath the canoe. "A skinny, wiggly thing," she said. "Deer and 'coons don't bother me, not even bears, only things that squirm. In London I 'ated to walk in the street after a rain because of all the worms—slimy, squishy worms."

"Worms can't hurt you," Amy said. "They don't have teeth."

"That's what everyone says, but I 'ate them. I feel sick." She shuddered again.

"It's the insects I don't like," Amy said. "I've killed a million of them." She squashed a crawling bug right there as it walked on her knee.

As the days slipped by, Amy bound more plants to her toe. Gradually the redness disappeared and the swelling went down. All sunburns had, at long last, finished peeling, and no animals got close enough to hurt anyone.

Tall, skinny birds with long, long necks, stark white against the dark forest, waded at the edge of the water. They dipped their bills in the mud and poked around for something to eat. The birds stretched their necks and pointed their beaks at the canopy while they swallowed the morsels they'd found.

Next day, what looked like a huge, brown, spotted cat jumped out of the trees. "Look how big he is," Amy said in a hoarse whisper. "Bigger than any cat I ever saw in London."

"An' look at 'is tail!" whispered Priscilla. "'Tis like 'e's only got 'alf 'a one."

"Do you suppose it has always been like that, or do you think another animal bit it off?" Sarah asked, sounding concerned.

"Don't know," Amy said. She shrugged.

The cat pounced on one of the white birds standing with water halfway up its skinny legs. A sudden fount of red spurted from the base of the bird's neck, and its head flopped over. The cat dragged it out of the water and ripped it to pieces. He ate the parts he wanted and left the beak and feet.

Priscilla leaned over the side of the canoe and vomited. Pieces of half-digested fish floated by the dugout. Amy gagged.

"Oh the poor bird," said Sarah.

After that, Virginia kept the dugout far enough from shore that it would be impossible for the cat, or anything else, to get to them.

Amy helped guide the canoe along any time Virginia would let her. As soon as evening shadows crept across the water, he cruised to shore and beached the dugout. Amy was thankful he did. The journey was scary enough when she could see. The thought of going through the swamp in the dark terrified her.

While he fished, Amy gathered twigs and grass and laid a fire on the sand like she had seen him do. She took the fire-starting sticks from the canoe and rubbed them together.

"It doesn't work for me," she said, exasperated. "The wood gets warm, but no smoke and no flame."

While Amy tried to light the fire, Priscilla used vines and small branches to make a rack on which to cook whatever Virginia speared, something all of the girls had learned to do by watching him.

When he returned with four fish, he snatched the sticks from Amy, and said, "No. Me make." He scowled at her.

Sarah immediately jumped behind her sister.

"Don't anger 'im," Priscilla warned. "If 'e thinks 'tis 'is job, let 'im do it. We don't want 'im to get upset and leave us in the forest."

"Perhaps I didn't do it right," Amy said. "He does it with such ease."

Virginia set the fish over the fire on Priscilla's rack, then took a roundish thing out of the canoe, collected oil dripping from the cooking fish, and rubbed it in his hair.

"That's how he makes it stand up!" Amy exclaimed. She looked at Priscilla and wrinkled her nose.

"Stinky," said Priscilla. "Fish oil."

Taking a chunk of charred wood from the fire, he mixed it with fish oil and repainted the black circles on his shoulders.

Amy raised both eyebrows at Priscilla, and Priscilla hid a giggle with her hand. Virginia cleaned the gourd with leaves and tossed it back into the canoe.

Every evening when the sun disappeared, Amy curled up on the sand, waiting for sleep. "You know, if someone from our ship has gone out to look for us, they'll never find us here," she said.

"Aye. They'll look along the seashore."

"What can we do? Which way is the sea?" asked Sarah.

Amy rose up on her elbows and looked directly at her sister, her mouth set in a straight line. "We can't go back. We stay with Virginia. He's the one who knows how to live in these woods."

Priscilla nodded and said, "I just wish I knew where we're headed."

Amy tried to snuggle into the dirt and found it impossible. Dirt was not soft. With the chorus of croaking frogs, she couldn't sleep. She heard growly noises and something snapped in the trees. The frogs instantly stopped croaking. Amy picked up a stick and waited to be attacked—nothing came.

As the journey continued, the water got shallower. Virginia exchanged his paddle for a longer, skinnier pole. He pushed it into the riverbed, expertly steering the canoe around stumps and fallen branches.

Five feathers now adorned Amy's hair. "The black ones look best," Priscilla told her, "if you put them next to a yellow one or a white one."

Now the water they traveled in was more of a bog than a creek. Huge trees grew out of it, and a constant smell of damp hung in the air. It made Amy's nose run. She wiped it on the back of her hand.

Huge lily pads floated on the surface. They looked a lot like ones Amy had seen in England afloat in the moat of a castle she had once visited. She pointed to one of them. "Look, Sarah. See the tiny frog?" A frog so small it could easily have sat on Amy's finger leaped from the green pad to the black water.

One of the tall, white birds put his head down and drew it back up with a little frog in its bill. "I hope that's not the same frog we saw," said Sarah, wiping away a tear.

Every night they made camp and cooked fish over the fire on a grill made of sticks. One night Amy sighed and said, "I wish I had an apple—a juicy, crunchy apple."

"Me, too," said Priscilla, "something besides fish. I'm tired of eating fish."

Sarah sighed. "I want to go where people are. If I can go without getting on one of those ships like the *Hope*, that is. I don't like it here. I wish we'd never left England."

Virginia handed Amy a fish, saying, "*Nammais.*"

"See? *Nammais* is his word for fish," Amy said.

"Either that or for eat." Priscilla put her fish on a leaf to let it cool before she bit into it.

"Wouldn't it be nice to have a fork to eat with?" Amy picked up a stick and pretended. It didn't work. The chunk of fish fell in the mud. She sloshed it off with water from her drinking gourd and ate it anyway.

Priscilla sat with her fish and looked miserable. "I don't like this awful mud we're always in," she said.

"The whole world has turned to mud. It'll be better when we get to Jamestown." Amy had no way of knowing that, or of knowing if Virginia was headed for Jamestown. She thought again he might be going to an Indian village.

"I'd like to see another city," Priscilla said, "a dirty, smelly, noisy city crowded with people, but 'ere in the New Land, so I don't 'ave to go on a ship. I don't want to go back to London. There's nothing good there."

A black snake slid off a log and wiggled over the mossy ground in front of her. She shuddered and threw a chunk of mud at it. The snake hissed, showing a throat as white as cotton.

Sarah screamed, like she did every time a snake came near.

The snake slithered away.

Amy still thought going back to England would be best, after she found her father, of course. She looked to where she saw a patch of night sky between the branches. The moon, which had been a sliver when they'd been shipwrecked, was now a round full globe. "I wish I could see London again," she said. "I want to see a street paved with cobblestones and a horse clopping down it. I don't care if I have to go on another ship. I'll get on one." She tossed her fish bones in the fire. "As soon as we find Father, I want to go."

"If we 'ave to be 'ere, I wish I 'ad something big to sleep on top of, or a 'ouse to get inside. I'm not used to being in the open like this. 'Tis scary. I 'ave always slept with walls around and a roof over."

"I want a real bed," Sarah said, "like in England, not a skinny hammock like on the ship. I can't sleep on this dirt."

"I can't either," Amy said. "It won't last forever. We'll get to people soon, Englishmen with houses and beds and dishes and forks."

She glanced at Virginia taking a drink from the gourd of rainwater he carried in the canoe. It rained every two or three days for a little bit, and he managed to collect enough in one of the bowls that none of them was ever thirsty. They could have drank the river water if they had to—the animals did.

When the rain poured down, Amy huddled with her gown over her head, trying to keep dry—an impossible task. One day Virginia didn't spear any fish for dinner. He tried, but there were none. Amy had only a few bites of leftover ones for evening meal. Her empty stomach growled as she threw chunks of wood on the fire. Thank goodness for the water.

While she drank, a gray fox came to the creek. It balanced on a log at the edge of the swamp and stretched over to sip the black water. "Isn't he pretty?" Amy whispered to Priscilla, nudging her. "Look how dainty he drinks, like a duchess."

"*Assimoest*," Virginia said.

"That must mean *fox*," Amy said. "I'm getting used to his words."

The fox had a silvery tail twice as bushy as any fuzzy cat Amy had seen in England. Something growled in the woods. As quick as lightning the fox popped his head up and bolted. Sarah cried out when that happened.

Amy never found out what had growled. She stayed awake that night, afraid whatever it was would dash out of the forest to eat her. Should somebody keep watch? Sarah squeezed between Amy and Priscilla, leaving Priscilla on the outside with the snakes.

At last the sun turned the clouds pink and peeked through the thick canopy of leaves to wake the girls and Virginia. Amy hadn't slept a wink.

"I'm so stiff and sore," she said when they'd started off again. "I move like an old, old lady. My arms don't hurt, but my legs and my back do. From sitting the same way day after day." She wiggled where she sat to relieve her back. "But we need to keep going no matter how much it hurts."

Priscilla nodded.

Now small roundish turtles sat up on logs and stumps in the water, sunning themselves in the tiny, thin, warm rays that filtered through the thick cover of branches. Amy nudged Priscilla, "They're about the size of a small teapot, different from the huge ones on the beach."

Priscilla flicked water at the turtle. It didn't move.

Amy lost track of the days. It seemed like a hundred. She didn't have anything to make marks on here like she'd had on the ship. "We've been in this forest forever," she said, tears prickling at her eyelids.

She and Priscilla continued to take turns poling that day, but the river got skinnier and skinnier. Sometimes she could hardly get the canoe around fallen stumps and logs in the water. Virginia hadn't caught a fish for two days now.

"What do we do if it gets so narrow we can't get through? What if we get stuck?" Priscilla said with a note of alarm.

"I've been wondering the same thing," Amy said. "No English people live here, no people at all. We haven't even seen any Indians. I thought he was going to a settlement."

"What if there is no settlement? Will we be here forever?" asked Sarah.

Amy didn't answer. She couldn't. The same question gnawed at her.

8 Into the Forest

When Amy opened her eyes next morning, Virginia was wading in the mud by the riverbank and spearing fish. While Priscilla collected wood, she laid grass and twigs on the ground in another attempt to build a cooking fire. Every day she'd kept at it, and at last she could lay one that pleased him. She hadn't succeeded in lighting it, though. Once or twice she'd tried, when he went off hunting and couldn't see. All that happened was the sticks got warm.

After they'd eaten the fish, he said, "Walk."

"Well, that answers the question of what we do when the river gets too narrow," Amy said.

"Aye. I wonder how far."

They carried the canoe, Virginia at the front, Amy and Priscilla at the back. Often they had to set it down so Virginia could cut brush away and make a proper path.

"Is this a trail?" Priscilla asked, ducking under a low branch.

Amy pushed her hair back. "Looks like it, overgrown, that's all."

Sarah reached for the knife. "I'll cut brush. If the journey will go faster, I shall help. I'm still a lady, though. Don't forget."

She went ahead and tried as best she could to clear a way through. But the only branches she could cut were the small ones. One of the others had to come and cut anything else.

Amy resisted the urge to say something rude. She didn't want Sarah to go back to refusing to do her share.

She found climbing over logs and pushing past brush was much worse than sitting in a canoe. In the canoe she got stiff and sore; when walking, the skinny branches cut her skin. "I never thought I'd want to be paddling again," Amy said through a scratchy branch that had hit her in the face.

"I 'ate this swamp," said Priscilla, panting.

Sarah couldn't clear everything. Many times they set the canoe down and helped her cut brush away before they could go on.

Vines twined around Amy's ankles as she tried to walk. All of the girls had their shoes and gowns back on. Amy's shoes were stiff and hard from their soaking in salt water. They rubbed blisters on her toes and heels. She switched them from one foot to the other, but it didn't help. Her feet hurt with each step because the shoes were now too small. "Perhaps the shoes wouldn't grate so if I still had my stockings," she said, "but they fell apart long ago." Nevertheless, Amy needed the shoes for the rough trail, so she gritted her teeth and kept quiet about it.

"I 'ave blisters, too," Priscilla said. "'Tis because my shoes are old ones that were once my mother's. They are too big and flop on my feet."

"You have even more raw places than I do," Amy said, looking at Priscilla's wounds.

Virginia scraped soft bark from a twig with his knife and handed it to Priscilla, saying *messetts* like he had before.

Priscilla took off her shoes and placed the shredded bark on the bloody spots.

"Why doesn't Virginia have trouble walking?" Amy asked while she nursed her swollen feet. "He keeps hiking with a spring in his step and doesn't suffer any cuts at all. And he's barefoot."

Priscilla cradled one of her mangled feet and said, "'E knows where to step, I s'pose."

Amy's gown dragged in the mud as she staggered along. She wished she could hold it up like Sarah, but she needed her hands to grip the canoe. It also meant her hands were not free to swat the insects that bit her at every step. While sitting in the canoe, she had swatted dozens of bugs.

When Sarah got an insect bite, it swelled and became tomato red. Virginia peeled off more of the same bark Amy had used on her feet for Sarah's welts.

"It makes them feel better," Sarah said. She tore lace from her petticoat, like Amy had, to hold the bark on her arms. But she couldn't tie it to her face. Amy heard her scratching all night long. By morning Sarah had a big lump below her ear that bled.

"I must put the canoe down and rest," Amy said after they'd been walking a few hours. She dropped her end and sat in the mud where she stood, puffing and panting to get her breath back.

Virginia paused with them.

"I can't stay upright." Amy moaned and hugged her knees.

Virginia sat behind her, back to back. He pointed around behind himself.

"I think 'e wants you to lean on 'im," said Priscilla.

Amy propped herself against Virginia, as if his back were a chair back. "Thank you," she said.

"T'ank 'oo," he copied.

"I'm so glad we met him," Amy said to Priscilla. "If we hadn't, we would be dead."

Priscilla swallowed.

After that, any time they took a break and sat in the mud, Amy leaned back-to-back against Virginia. Priscilla rested against Sarah the same way. It made the journey easier to bear when held up by someone else. "He always knows exactly what to do to make the trip endurable," Amy said.

From dawn till dark they slogged in the mud, carrying the canoe through the thick underbrush and buzzing insects. Amy lost count of how many days they'd been walking. She thought only about putting one foot in front of the other.

"For days and days the trees have been green," she said. "Now some have turned brown or yellow and some leaves have fallen. Perhaps it's October."

Each night was colder than the last, making sleep impossible. Amy cuddled with Sarah and Priscilla when she did try. "At last the insects have disappeared," she said.

"They've gone to bed for the winter," said Sarah.

Amy snorted. "That's the only good thing about cold nights."

"I don't blame them," Priscilla said. "Wish I could, but I can do nothing." She wiped a tear away with her finger, leaving a patch of mud beneath her eye.

Amy tried to use dry leaves, like Virginia did, to cover herself when she slept. It wasn't much warmer.

"My hair is so tangled and my gown so torn, I know I don't look like an English girl anymore," she said when she woke up.

Priscilla nodded. "You look like a wild person. I'm sure I do, too."

When the ribbons the girls had used to bind their braids fell apart, Virginia cut vines to make new ones. Priscilla and Sarah redid each other's hair. Amy, though, had to let hers fall. It was too snarled to braid.

Some days Virginia wasn't able to shoot anything, so while Amy and Priscilla worked on the fire, he went to the edge of the forest and dug under vines growing there. He returned to the girls carrying fat, oval-shaped roots, pointed at both ends. He coated them with mud and tossed them into the coals of the fire Amy tended. The roots baked while Amy's stomach growled. He used two sticks to fish them out and passed one to each girl. After washing the mud off at a stream, Virginia bit into his. As soon as her root cooled enough, Amy washed it and tasted it, too.

"It's like a potato," she said.

One day as the sun started to set, she saw water sparkling through the trees.

Virginia put his end of the canoe down. "Sleep," he said, like he always did when they stopped for the night. He went hunting with his bow and arrow and came back with a rabbit.

"Fish and rabbit, fish and rabbit, fish and rabbit." Amy groaned. "I'd like something different. Why doesn't he shoot one of those deer that are always peeking at us?"

"Perhaps because we'd 'ave to carry it with us, and 'tis all we can 'andle with the canoe." Priscilla dropped her armload of wood.

Sarah nodded. She collected sticks and vines for Priscilla to make a rack on which to cook the rabbit. They got no more arguments from Sarah about helping with the work. Amy assumed her sister could tell every hand was needed.

"I don't want to eat rabbit again." Priscilla tied sticks together with the vines Sarah collected.

"I don't either," said Amy. "I want beef stew with carrots and onions."

But she ate the rabbit, then wrapped the leftover meat in her petticoat to save for the next day. Her petticoat smelled like smoked fish and grease now, and she knew if she ever got to a settlement, she'd burn it.

When they got to the distant water, Amy tasted it to make sure it was the sea. Good, salty! Off on the horizon, to her right, a ship with sails billowing sailed away from her.

"Our ship!" Priscilla exclaimed. "The 'ope."

"A ship, anyway." Amy's heart raced.

Sarah jumped up and down then turned to run down the beach. "Let's wave to them."

Amy and Priscilla pulled her back.

"You said before you'd never again get on a ship," Amy said.

"I don't want to get on it, but that doesn't mean I don't want people around me I can talk to."

"The ship might not be English." Priscilla frowned. She squinted and shaded her eyes. "Perhaps 'tis Spanish. I can't see a flag."

Amy watched the ship, but never found out what nation it belonged to, or its name either. She kept her eyes on it as it sailed over the curve of the earth out of sight.

Sarah started to cry. "There isn't anybody to help us." She sobbed. "Nobody. We're all alone and lost with a savage Indian and a lot of animals that want to eat us." She stuck her dirty thumb in her mouth.

"Virginia keeps saying 'English'," Amy pointed out, trying to cheer up her sister. "He's taking us somewhere where they have people we'll be able to talk to."

Priscilla nodded, chewing on the ends of her fingers where her nails used to be.

Virginia held up two fingers. He pointed at the sky and said, "*Ninge*. Two suns. English." Then he smiled.

"Does he mean it's two more suns till we get to English people?" Amy held up two fingers, too. She pointed to the fingers and said, "*Ninge*" like he did.

He nodded, held up one finger and said, "*Nekut*," the second finger and said, "*ninge*."

"Aye. *Nekut, ninge*," said Priscilla. "One, two."

All that day they paddled on the sea. No trees shaded them here, so Amy worked with the sun beating on her back. She dipped in, pushed the water behind, pulled the paddle back out, and began all over. She kept at it until the sun disappeared.

When she looked off into the distance, she thought she saw smoke. "What is that?" she asked Priscilla, who was now taking a turn with the paddle.

"Maybe a cloud." Priscilla took another stroke.

Priscilla had seen it right. Clouds were building on the horizon. The wind came up. It pushed the sea into rolling waves and then into angry ones that threw the tiny craft every which way. No matter how hard they paddled, they made no headway. It seemed to Amy they even went backward. While she worked with her paddle, a drop of rain splashed in her face.

"Go." Virginia pointed to shore.

Amy turned the dugout toward the beach. "Thank goodness. If this is to be an enormous storm, like the one on the *Hope*, I don't want to be out on the ocean in this tiny canoe."

As they neared the sand, Sarah stood to get out. "No! Sarah. You'll tip us," Amy yelled. The canoe tilted and Sarah lost her balance. She plunged over the side into the murky water and disappeared below.

Amy jumped after her, balancing with difficulty because of the waves. She dug her toes into the sandy bottom.

The only other time Amy had had her face all the way under the water was while floating on the mast. Now it stung her eyes and choked her as the waves had then.

But she didn't hesitate. Somewhere under the surface Sarah was drowning. Amy hung onto the canoe with one hand and squatted, eyes wide open. She couldn't see because the waves stirred up the sand. All of a sudden she felt Sarah's foot. She grabbed the ankle and hung on. Lungs aching for air, she pulled Sarah toward her and tried to stand.

When her head broke the surface, she gasped in a huge lung full of air. "Help," she yelled. "Help me."

Virginia plunged into the sea. He came up sputtering and grasping Sarah under her arms. He staggered to shore and laid her on the sand face down. She didn't look to be breathing. Virginia pushed on Sarah's back until water gushed out of her mouth.

Sarah coughed and vomited more water. She coughed four more times, then cried. Hearing Sarah cry this time was like music to Amy's ears. It meant Sarah could breathe.

"I'm all right now," Sarah managed to choke out between the coughing, the vomiting, and the sobs.

Virginia smiled. "Sarah *winganouse*. Good now. *Winganouse*." He picked her up and carried her away from the surf. Amy and Priscilla hauled the canoe onto the beach.

He propped the dugout at both ends to make a little hut. All of them huddled under it without a fire. No remnants of food had survived when the canoe tipped.

With her soaking wet head resting on her knees, Amy huddled under the canoe all night long, her feet pulled up out of the rain.

"This storm is not as furious as the one on the 'ope," Priscilla said, teeth chattering.

"It is as wet." A rivulet of muddy water flowed under the canoe past Amy's feet. She twitched her skirt out of it, but was too tired to move her feet. Leaning against Virginia, and with Priscilla doing the same against Sarah, she knew she had never been colder.

Amy awoke at first light to the chirping of birds. She took her turn paddling along the shore that day and thought she saw smoke again. This time, though, she kept her silence.

But Sarah didn't. "I think you were right before, Amy. I think I saw smoke like you did."

"I see it, too," Amy said. "I didn't want to say anything until I was close enough to smell it."

Virginia pointed and said, "Fire."

"I 'ope it is Jamestown, not a Spanish place."

Amy nodded. "And I hope Father is here to greet us. I can't wait to see him, and your mother, too, of course. And I want to see our ship anchored out front."

"We won't," Sarah said. "It would have gone back to England by now. But it sank."

Amy glared at her.

They paddled for what seemed forever. At long last, when the sun started to sink, Amy saw the place the smoke came from. "Houses," she said. Her heart raced. "Wooden ones built like English houses—lots of them."

"And ships," Priscilla said. She sounded as excited as Amy felt. "Ships with English flags anchored out front in the water."

Virginia beached the canoe and the three girls stood on the sand next to it.

"At last, a real town, not a dead one like the ghost colony." Amy saw people walking on the shore. She smiled for the first time in weeks. Crossing her fingers, Amy prayed she'd find her father here.

Part 2
The Colony

The Settlement

A crowd collected on shore. Amy tried to catch sight of her father, but he wasn't there. The people stared back. They must have seen the canoe come in. So many people had gathered on the beach, she thought it might be everyone in town.

Virginia grinned and said, "Hello." He put his hand out in a greeting, too, the way an Englishman would to shake hands.

Folks standing on the sand acted like they knew him, and a man with curly white hair came up to grasp his hand. "Hello," the man said back to Virginia, stretching over a wide-eyed boy to reach.

Amy took in the whole scene with Priscilla clinging to her on one side and Sarah the other. She peered at each person. Where was her father? Someone said, "Who are they?" in English. This must be an English settlement.

"Are you English people?" Amy asked, wanting to make sure. "Is this Jamestown?"

"It is," the curly haired man confirmed. "It is Jamestown. And who are you? Wherever did you come from?"

"From England. On a ship." Amy waved her arm at the ocean.

Virginia stood in the background and watched.

Amy wondered what these people thought of her since she didn't have her cap. Mother had always said a girl must never go outside the house without one. Sarah fished hers from the front of her gown and crammed it on her head. It was the same color as the mud in the swamp and looked like it had never been white.

Amy began picking out the feathers she had stuck in her hair throughout the trip. She dropped them to the beach. Dozens of them were snarled there to remove.

Priscilla stood chewing her fingers and looking at the sand.

People on shore muttered to each other. One woman puckered her nose and said, "They're dirty."

"Did they come all the way from England in that tiny canoe?" another asked. "They must have been frightened."

A man said, "Did they come by themselves? Three girls alone like that?"

"We got caught in a storm," Priscilla said, not much louder than a whisper. "When the ship broke apart, the mast snapped off and we 'ung on to it."

Amy added, "Did the *Hope* come in here? That is our ship, the *Hope*. Where is my father? Solomon Purdy?"

A wrinkled woman with hair the color of smoke nodded and said, "I 'ave 'eard tell of that ship." The woman wore black and only three teeth showed when she talked. "I 'aven't seen it, though."

"I've heard of it, too," said a man. "Folks said it sank." The man looked as wrinkled and had as many teeth missing as the woman.

Sarah sobbed and stuck her filthy thumb in her mouth.

Why is she crying? Amy wondered. *She's the one who has been saying all along that it sank.*

"It didn't come in 'ere," the woman in the black gown said. "We 'aven't seen it." She turned to the man beside her, the man with the curly hair, and shrugged.

"There's talk of a ship found to the south of us, on a beach, no name though," the man said. He removed his pipe from between his teeth and coughed. "Come to think of it, it was a year ago."

Amy knew they had not been lost for a year.

Another man shook his head and muttered, "I 'aven't seen anybody named Purdy."

Amy clutched Priscilla and Sarah and now they all cried. "If the ship did sink, we have no parents at all. No mother, no father. Nobody," she managed to choke out. "What should we do?" She wiped her nose on her grimy sleeve.

"My mother was the only family I 'ad in the 'ole world," Priscilla said. "We're—all of us—alone."

"Maybe some got rescued," said Amy.

"They didn't," the old man with hardly any teeth said. "We'd hear if they did. They'd show up somewhere. You girls are the first we've seen, and you must have been lost for weeks by the looks of you."

"Now, Josiah, you can't say for sure it vanished," the woman in black said. "Sometimes ships show up long after they're due. Or maybe the people 'ave been rescued by a different ship and taken back to England."

"Or Spain," said Josiah. "In chains."

A man who had no lines on his young face and not much hair on top of his head said, "Yes. If the people were picked up by a Spanish ship, they'd be put in prison and held for ransom."

Amy fought back tears.

Sarah sobbed without ceasing.

Priscilla chewed her nails.

"It's possible they came in safely somewhere," Amy muttered.

"I 'ope you are right." Priscilla shook her head. She didn't sound like she believed it.

The sun had almost disappeared when the woman in black took charge. "I am 'enrietta Ford," she said. "You girls come 'ome with me till we decide what to do with you. I 'ave stew left from our evening meal. You look 'ungry. You may call me Mistress Ford." She furrowed her brow and wrinkled her nose. "You all need a bath."

"Who is she?" Amy whispered to Priscilla.

Priscilla shrugged.

"We must go with her. What else can we do? I don't wish to camp on any more beaches, not for the rest of my life." Amy longed to be in a house with walls and a roof and a fireplace—any house at all.

"What does Virginia do?" she asked, gesturing toward him.

And Sarah added, "Is there an Indian village close by?"

Amy knew a wild man from the forest would not go to a proper English house.

"D'ya mean the savage? He will sleep on the shore," Henrietta Ford said. "That is what the savages always do. Come along, girls."

Amy gave Virginia a hug before she left him, hearing a chorus of muttering from the crowd as she did. "Good-bye, my friend."

Virginia hugged her back. "*Netab*," he said, "good-bye." More muttering.

"*Netab*," Amy said. She assumed it meant friend. "Thank you."

Several onlookers raised their eyebrows and muttered to each other. Amy didn't care. He had been her companion for weeks, and she had learned he was her friend. She wasn't sure how many weeks they had been traveling, but knew it was many. Father had been lost. Mother was gone. She didn't want to lose Virginia, too.

Priscilla and Sarah each gave him a hug as well, then went with Amy as she followed Mistress Ford past the rows of wooden structures lining the waterfront. Some of them were stores, some houses. All were new, and none had stone any higher than the foundation. A thick forest of needle leaf trees loomed behind the town.

"Not near as many buildings as we left back in London," Priscilla said. "London goes on for miles and miles."

Amy nodded. "Father said London now has two hundred thousand people." She walked on a roadway of dirt, no cobblestones like streets in England. Walking was easier, however, than it had been in the forest.

"Is this lady a witch?" Sarah whispered. "She looks like one. I think she is."

"Hush. She'll hear you." But Amy wondered about that herself. The lady looked old and she wore black. Amy had always heard witches were old and wore black.

Henrietta Ford lived close to the end of the second row of buildings, way past the middle of town where they had landed the canoe. As soon as Amy entered the house, she smelled smoke. For past weeks fires had been outdoors where it drifted away—not here, walls kept it in. The dim room held a rocking chair and a rug in front of the fireplace, a table to the left of the door, a cupboard beside that, and not much more.

Mistress Ford took a splinter from the woodbox, touched it to a burning log in the fireplace, and used that to light three candles on the table. "Sit 'ere," she said, and pointed to a bench. "I'll get you some supper." She tossed the splinter into the fire.

That evening Amy ate her first English meal in more than a month. Mistress Ford had finished eating, but she still had stew in a pot hanging from a pothook in the huge brick fireplace. She had bread to go with the stew, real bread, and butter. On the ship Amy had eaten stale, moldy biscuits. Before she could bite into one, she'd had to pick out nasty little bugs.

"What is the meat?" she asked.

"Venison," Mistress Ford answered.

Ah. Deer meat. It could have been any kind, and she would have eaten it. At least it wasn't fish or rabbit. She had eaten venison lots of times. Her father often hunted in England.

Amy sat at the homemade table and ate until her stomach hurt. She couldn't get enough gravy. She poured it over bread and ate it that way. Delicious. She was happy to have bread she could bite into. She'd always thought she might break a tooth on one of those rock-hard ship's biscuits. Many people did. Sarah sat across from her and ate two whole potatoes and heaps of carrots, besides the meat. Priscilla wolfed down two helpings of everything.

"May I take Virginia a piece of bread?" Amy asked Mistress Ford when she'd finished. She pointed to the loaf on the table. "Perhaps he has never tasted it."

"Is that your friend the savage?" Mistress Ford asked, slicing off a thick portion.

"Yes ma'am."

Mistress Ford buttered the slice, then reached for a crock with something red in it. "'Ere. We'll put preserves on it. They're good. Though I shouldn't say since I made them myself." She smeared on red fruit with a few big lumps that looked like they could be strawberries. She handed the slice to Amy.

Taking the bread, Amy smiled a thank you to Mistress Ford and left to give it to Virginia. Someone as nice as Mistress Ford couldn't be a witch, Amy had decided, even someone old who wore black. Amy had never heard of a witch who made preserves.

Priscilla and Sarah walked to the beach with her. Amy wondered if she'd be able to find Virginia in the dark, but he'd built a fire. It was a good thing. The half moon gave little light. Since she had plunged into the Atlantic on the mast, she had seen a whole moon cycle and now part of another. It must be close to the middle of October.

"English food," she said as she handed Virginia the slice. "You looked after us for such a long time. I wanted to do something for you." She noticed he already had a fish broiling on a rack.

"'Tis bread," Priscilla said. "English bread. You made us Indian meals."

Virginia hesitated a moment, then took the slice. He looked puzzled and stuck out his tongue to taste the fruit. "Good," he said. He took a huge bite. "Good."

"It's preserves," Sarah explained, "bread and preserves."

"Bread 'n p'serves," Virginia repeated.

Amy, Priscilla, and Sarah left him on the chilly shore and returned to Mistress Ford's cozy home.

As Amy came in from the street, a man came in the back door. Mistress Ford introduced him as Mister Ford. He had mostly gray hair, a gray mustache, and a little pointed gray beard. The beard and mustache looked like portraits Amy had seen of former King James, except King James's beard and mustache looked all brown. England didn't have James anymore. Now the king was Charles. He had long, curling, black hair—a periwig for sure.

"Call me Mister William," the man said when Mistress Ford introduced him. He was chewing on a sliver of wood. "We are not so old-fashioned 'ere in the New Country as folks are in England. Mister Ford sounds stuffy." He turned to Mistress Ford. "They aren't going to stay 'ere, are they? We 'ave so little room."

Mistress Ford shook her head. "We'll take them to the town meeting tomorrow. Someone will want three girls to work."

She had a washtub filled with hot water for the girls to bathe in. A screen of quilts had been hung from the rafters around the tub. Priscilla and Sarah wrapped up in other quilts to keep warm while waiting their turn.

Amy stood in the tub and dipped water over herself. It felt warm and soothed her sore muscles. The tub wasn't large enough to sit down in, although she thought Sarah and Priscilla would be able to when their turns came.

"We 'ave to make you acceptable," Mistress Ford said, handing Amy a cake of soap, "so young folks will want to give you an 'ome."

Amy scrubbed off the grime of all those weeks, then kneeled and leaned over the tub to wash her hair.

Sarah stepped into the water as Amy got out. And Amy wrapped up in a quilt while she raked at her tangled hair with a metal comb.

Mistress Ford kept busy the whole time. She dipped dirty water out of the tub, dumped it out the door, then refilled the tub with hot water from the pot hanging in the fireplace.

Mister William picked up the gowns. "I'll take these outside, 'Attie," he said to Mistress Ford, "an' clean the mud off of 'em." Out he went, taking a large brush, like the kind you might use on a horse, with him.

All the time Amy worked on those knots in her hair, she heard Mister William outside beating and brushing the gowns.

When he brought the gowns back in he said, "'Tis the best I can do. I'm off to the shore now to see 'oos fire that is."

"I know," said Amy. "It's Virginia's, our Indian friend." But Mister William had gone and didn't hear her.

Mistress Ford put the gowns, shifts, and petticoats in the pot Amy and the other girls had used for bathing and scrubbed them hard. She hung the pot over the fire and boiled the gowns. She scoured them with the same strong smelling soap the girls had used for bathing. "The soil does not come out," she said, tut-tutting the whole time.

Amy's fancy petticoat with the ruffle and what was left of the lace fell apart before she got a chance to burn it like she'd said she would.

After dipping up muddy water from the tub and dumping it out the back door three times, then refilling the pot with fresh hot water, Mistress Ford wrung the gowns out. "That's all I can do," she said. "Now you girls each 'old your own frock in front of the fire. Wave it back and forth. 'Twill dry faster."

Amy did as Mistress Ford said. In England a maid had laundered her clothes. The only place she had ever seen anybody do it, was on the ship. There, her father paid Priscilla's mother to wash for them. But washing clothes in salt water did little to get them clean. And mud that wouldn't come out had discolored Amy's gown, Sarah's, too. The soil didn't show up on Priscilla's dark frock.

"Ahhhhh. Those gowns look some better now," Henrietta Ford said when at last they had dried enough to put back on.

But Amy knew she and Sarah needed new gowns. Sarah had grown, and though not so mud-stained as Amy's, Sarah's gown now showed her ankles.

Mistress Ford and Mister William didn't have any extra beds. The whole house was one big room. Amy, Priscilla, and Sarah were to sleep on the rag rug in front of the fire. The Fords said their good nights and climbed a ladder to their own bed in a loft over the main room.

It must have been close to midnight when Amy sat hugging her knees like she had when she'd sat before the fire in the forest. Here, no scary animals screeched in the night and, for a change, it wasn't cold.

"It's a cozy house," she whispered to Priscilla, still tugging at the knots in her hair with the comb. "I've never before seen a house with only one room, not ever in my whole life."

"I 'ave," Priscilla whispered back. "I 'ave seen many."

"We don't have beds," Sarah pointed out. "I could sleep better if I had one."

Amy kept at the remaining tangles. "Too bad we can't stay here till we find Father," she said. "I would like it here." A tear squeezed out of her eye. She wiped it on the quilt. But Mistress Ford and Mister William had made it clear they were too old for girls. It seemed they didn't want young people around at all, and the house was small.

She must find Father. Where could he be? Had he landed on a beach somewhere? Perhaps he was struggling through that same wilderness she and Priscilla and Sarah had fought so long to get through. How would Father get food? How would he know which way to go? Would he step on one of those nasty black snakes with a mouth as white as the cliffs of Dover? Those snow-white cliffs had been Amy's last glimpse of her homeland.

She felt her life may as well be ended. "We have found English people," Amy said in a voice that could barely be heard, "but we are still as lost as we were in the forest."

Town Meeting

Amy awakened to sounds of Mistress Ford stoking the fire and stirring something in an iron pot. She stretched, put her stained gown back on, then sat at the family table ready for another English meal, morning meal this time.

Priscilla and Sarah had awakened, too. When Amy saw Priscilla folding her quilt, she got up from the table to fix her own. She hadn't thought of making her bed.

The same as when they'd first started their journey in the forest, Sarah sat back and let others do the work.

Amy stood with her hands on her hips. "Do yours," she ordered.

Sarah shook her head. "Not me. Why doesn't she have a maidservant?"

"Not everybody 'as one." Priscilla stowed the quilt she had folded in the big chest in the corner, then reached for Sarah's.

"You worked while we traveled." Amy gave her own quilt a final fold. "Why is it different here?"

"I had to then because I wanted to get to other people. I don't have to do it here. I can be a lady again."

Amy turned her back on her sister. "You're so haughty. Pride is a sin."

Sarah glared.

As well as oatmeal spooned up from the pot, Mistress Ford took a paddle with small yellowish cakes on it out of a door in the side of the fireplace. Amy figured the door led to an oven.

She picked up one of the cakes and sniffed it. "What is this?" she asked.

"Cornbread. Eating corn is something we learned from the savages. We grow our own on a bit of a farm we've got in back."

Amy put lots of butter on her cornbread. She'd never had anything made out of corn before. In fact, she didn't know what corn was. The butter melted and soaked in. Delicious. She ate four servings.

"Mmmmm. Good." Priscilla reached for another portion.

"Eat up," Mister William said while he downed his oatmeal. "We must get to the meeting and find an 'ome for each of you girls."

A home for each of them? Did that mean they'd all go to different families? "Can't we find out where our ship came in?" Amy asked. "Perhaps it didn't sink. Father will be looking for us." Thinking about living somewhere without Sarah and Priscilla panicked Amy. They needed each other. If she could find Father, or Priscilla's mother, they could be a family together.

"It sank," Mister William said. "All of the people are gone. No one was saved." Mister William shook his head. "'Tis a tragedy."

"Now you don't know that for sure," Mistress Ford said.

"Well...I s'pose it does no 'arm to wish for other survivors." Mister William stirred his coffee.

Sarah choked when she swallowed her mouthful of oatmeal. "I told you it sank, Amy. I told you." Sarah started to cry again. "I want my father."

"We'll find a nice family for you," Mistress Ford said. She patted Sarah's hand. "And we'll keep looking for 'im."

Sarah pulled her hand away.

Mistress Ford didn't seem to notice that Sarah pulled away. She continued, "Families for all of you. Lots of people need girls to work. We don't need girls 'ere. Mister William 'as a forge and makes things out of iron. 'E makes nails and tools and fancy things—weather vanes, candlesticks, 'inges for boxes and doors. 'Tisn't girl's work. 'E 'as a boy 'oo works for 'im."

"An' 'e's late," Mister William said, as if all of a sudden he'd realized it.

The back door opened and a boy swaggered in. He sat at the table across from Amy. Mistress Ford introduced him. "This is Charles. 'E came over from England to be indentured to Mister William and learn the iron trade. 'E 'as already been 'ere three of the eight years 'e'll be with us all told." She waved her hand toward the back of the house. "'E sleeps in a room by the forge."

Charles sneered at Amy and she wondered if he thought she wasn't worth looking at. He had yellow hair and more freckles than Amy had ever seen on any one person. He looked about the same age as Virginia, fourteen or fifteen perhaps. She smiled at him.

"I have the same name as the king," Charles said, his nose in the air as if having the same name as the king made him better than others.

I don't like him, Amy thought. *He thinks he's the best.* Mister William still talked about what to do with the girls. "Maybe a tobacco planter will want a girl to work," he said. Amy wondered what he meant by that. What was a tobacco planter? And how did you work tobacco? Because her father had smoked a pipe, she knew what it was. She looked at Priscilla and raised her eyebrows.

Priscilla returned the look.

"Girls are no use for working," Charles muttered through a mouthful of oatmeal. "Gentry girls can't do anything."

Amy glared at him.

Mister William got up from the table and reached for his hat. "You stoke the fire for me, Charles. We'll be back straight away."

As soon as she got outside and could see the seashore, Amy tried to catch sight of Virginia. She wanted to take him some cornbread. But he and his canoe were gone.

"Where is our Indian friend?" she asked Mistress Ford. "I thought he was to camp on the beach."

"Left early this morning, no doubt," Mistress Ford said.

Mister William pulled the door shut behind him. "Those savages don't stay around civilized folk too much. They think we live all wrong. Our 'ouses. Our clothes. What we eat. They'd rather be with their own kind doing things their own way."

"I didn't think he'd leave without a proper good-bye." Amy was grateful she had met Virginia. He wasn't a savage. He had shown her how to live in this New Land. Sometimes the Indian ways of doing things were better. She wondered if he had gone back to that beach where they'd seen the turtles on their first day.

"Is he coming here again?" Sarah asked. "I want him to."

"Aye. I do, too," said Priscilla.

"Perhaps," Mister William said. "We 'ave lots of savages lurking around wanting to trade things. Yours 'as been 'ere before. They trade furs and food—corn, fish, game, for things we 'ave that came from England. They're fond of knives, mirrors, whistles and toys, pots and pans. They really fancy scissors."

"Everything from tablecloths to teapots," Mistress Ford added. "They wear the tablecloths as if they were shawls."

"I want a canoe like Virginia's," said Sarah. "Do you think they would trade me one?"

Amy laughed. "You want a canoe? What do you have to offer them? Trade means you have to give something, too, you know."

"Aye. We 'ave nothing but the clothes we are wearing, and they're stained and torn. We can't even get 'em clean. Mistress Ford tried."

Amy continued walking with the Fords until she came to a big open space between the buildings that looked to be in the middle of town. Beside the first row of buildings, next to the river, she noticed a wall of tall poles set side by side.

"What is the fence for?" Amy asked.

"The posts? 'Tis the fort," Mister William told her. "We all go and 'ide in it if the savages attack."

"Have they ever done that? I thought they were friendly."

"Some are. Some aren't. We got attacked a while back. You never know, they might come again."

Amy remembered the ghost colony with dirt scraped up to make a wall around a huge dent in the ground. She'd thought it might be a castle. Perhaps that was a fort, too. Maybe the Indians weren't so friendly in that place. They might have had a battle with the colonists and taken them away somewhere as prisoners.

"What is the water called?" she asked. She thought of the river in London called the Thames and the ocean they had crossed to get to the New Land, the Atlantic.

"'Tis the James River."

Named after the old king, Amy assumed.

Lots of people had gathered in the open space. They talked and laughed together. This must be the town meeting.

When Amy arrived with Priscilla, Sarah, and the Fords, the people stopped talking and looked them over.

"Did you live in London?" a lady asked.

Priscilla nodded.

"No, ma'am," said Amy.

A man in a white wig stepped to the front of the group and the crowd silenced. He cleared his throat and waved his arms for attention. He had on a wide lace collar and fancy high-heeled shoes like Amy's father always wore.

"Sir John Jaret," Mister William said. "He runs things."

Henrietta Ford spoke up right away before Sir John could say anything to get the meeting started. "May I say something, sir? These girls need someone to live with." She put her hand on Amy's head then Sarah's. Priscilla's she couldn't reach. "They came up on our shore last night and have no families."

Sir John looked over the crowd. "Who will give these innocent girls a home?"

"I have no extra food on my table," a woman muttered.

A man Mistress Ford identified as a tobacco planter viewed Amy with scorn from beneath black eyebrows so bushy they met in the middle. "I like boys to work for me," the planter said. He sneered. "Boys are stronger. They are better at hoeing plants. Maybe I could take one girl to worm the leaves."

Amy lowered her voice and said to Mistress Ford, "What does he mean, worm the leaves?"

"A girl to walk up and down the rows and pick fat tobacco worms off of the plants," Mistress Ford whispered back. "Then to squish the worms under 'er 'eel and kill 'em."

Amy gagged, horrified.

Priscilla gagged too, and she shuddered.

The planter grabbed Priscilla's arm. "This one will do," he said. "The others look like gentry girls in those fancy dresses. They wouldn't want to be wormers."

Amy was shocked. He was right. She didn't want to pick worms off plants and she didn't want Priscilla to have to do it, either. Priscilla would be scared to death to touch a tobacco worm, whatever that was.

Priscilla started to sob. She looked at the ground.

No crops grew close to Jamestown that Amy could see. So she assumed tobacco didn't either. Priscilla might have to live far away. They wouldn't be able to visit each other. Amy's mother had died. Now Father was missing. She didn't want to lose Priscilla as well. She and Priscilla were friends. What did it matter if Priscilla wasn't a gentry girl? Class had no meaning in this harsh land.

She grabbed Priscilla's other arm and pulled her away from the tobacco farmer. Sticking her chin out, she said, "We stay together."

The planter shook his head and shrugged. "Makes no difference to me. I don't want girls anyway. Someone else will have to take them." He let go of Priscilla. "Boys are better. I was trying to help, that's all." He spit into the dirt.

Amy, Priscilla, and Sarah huddled close together and said nothing.

The planter continued. "Perhaps I'll wait for a ship from the Indies and buy a darky. Those Africans can't leave when they want to get married. They're with you for life." He sauntered away.

Sir John looked over the group. He cleared his throat. "These poor girls have no place to live," he said. "Surely there is room in your hearts and your homes for them."

The townspeople stood and muttered. They looked anywhere but at the girls or Sir John.

After some minutes a woman with hair the color of a carrot spoke up. "Can any of you girls sew? Can you make a gown?" she asked Amy.

Amy shook her head. "I've done my sampler. I'm good at roses. Sarah's working on hers. I can't make anything, though. I could never make a gown. In England we had a servant to sew."

"Pity. I could use a girl to help me in my tailoring shop." The lady pointed across the street. Amy saw a sign down a narrow side street with a needle and thread on it. The lady turned to walk away.

That's right in town, Amy realized. "Wait!" she shouted, giving Priscilla a little push toward the lady. "Priscilla can sew.

She sewed on the ship. She can make things." Amy didn't know if Priscilla could make a whole gown or not, but she supposed she could, or perhaps learn how. If Priscilla went to live with this lady, they could still visit.

"What is your name, child?" the lady asked.

"Priscilla Johnson, ma'am," Priscilla answered, her head down like she was speaking to the dirt.

"Is she right? You can sew? What kind do you do?"

Priscilla lifted her head and spoke a little louder. "Aye, 'tis true. My mother taught me. She was a seamstress 'oo took in work for people unable to do it themselves, or those 'oo didn't want to. 'Tis 'ow we made our money to buy food. I put on the buttons and did the 'ems for her."

"I think you could help me now," the lady said. "My name is Charity Stowe. You may call me Mistress Charity. Get your things and come home with me."

"I don't 'ave any things." Priscilla looked back at Amy and Sarah as Mistress Charity led her off.

Amy gave a small wave with her fingertips and watched her only friend in this New Land walk away. She'd miss her, but she was glad Priscilla had a place to live.

Sir John smiled. "And now these other two." But nobody offered. The townspeople continued to look at the ground, each other, the shore. Some of them left the meeting altogether.

A man mumbled, "Look at their frocks, lace and ruffles, gentry girls. They can't work."

"Let's go, 'Attie," Mister William said, a look of disgust on his face. "Let's go back to the forge. You shouldn't 'ave brought 'em 'ome in the first place."

"I 'ad to. They 'ad nowhere to go."

Gentry girls were useless, Amy realized. What would happen to her and to Sarah? Could they live in the woods like the Indians? They'd done that for weeks and weeks. But Amy knew it would be impossible without Virginia.

She thought of her Aunt Elizabeth and Uncle Edward far off across the ocean. They had a huge warm home with a fireplace in every room. She remembered she and her cousin Edmund had been good friends. "I think when another ship comes in, we should get on it and go back to England," Amy said to Sarah while they walked along. "Father will go there when he is rescued, if he can't come here. We must wait for word from him with Uncle Edward and Aunt Elizabeth."

Sarah shook her head. "Not me," she said through her sobs. "I'm never getting on another one of those horrid ships, not as long as I live. I'd rather die here."

"You may do that then," Amy said, feeling as disheartened as Sarah looked.

She knew they didn't have any money for their passage. You always had to pay. How could she get money? Or could she find Virginia and live with him?

It would be forever before she got those horses her father had promised when they'd left England such a long, long time ago. But she would gladly do without the horses, if she could have Father back.

Amy Helps

Back in the Fords' house, Amy tried to think of some way to earn a fair wage. If she could, she would be able to pay passage back to England for herself and Sarah. She wouldn't have to look for someone to give them a home. Putting up with a ship again wouldn't be so bad. She could do it. She'd make Sarah come, too, even if Sarah didn't want to. She'd make her.

Amy had seen people sweep a floor before, so she took the broom and tried her best. Maybe she could help someone in their home, be a housemaid. She was willing to work. Hadn't she worked all that time they'd traveled in Virginia's canoe? She'd almost learned how to be an Indian.

She glanced at her sister sitting in the rocking chair by the fireplace with her thumb stuck in her mouth. Sarah would never help earn money. Amy opened the door to sweep the bits and pieces outside.

"No, no," Mistress Ford corrected her, "in the fire. Everything will burn up. We don't waste fuel." She took the dustpan and showed Amy how to do it.

Amy asked, "Shall I get water from the well for you?" Everybody needed water.

"That would be too 'eavy. Mister William or I will get it," Mistress Ford said. She patted Amy's hand. "Gentry girls don't carry water. I know."

"I can do it," Amy said. "I'm strong. I can work. I don't want to be a gentry girl anymore. I don't want people to feel sorry for me."

"Let me get it," Mistress Ford said. She went outside with the bucket.

Back inside, she got her needles and thread and searched around where she kept the dish towels.

"Now what are you doing?" Amy asked.

"At least I am able to make new caps for you girls out of these tea towels if they're not too worn. That much I can do. When the next ship comes in, I shall get cloth to make frocks. 'Tis bound to 'ave some."

Amy watched while Mistress Ford sewed the caps. What a fast worker she was!

Mistress Ford continued, "I didn't plant any flax this year, or cotton either, so I'm not able to make the cloth myself, didn't think I'd need it. Next year a lot of people will plant cotton. I shall, too. You girls will be living somewhere else by then."

At the end of the day, Amy and Sarah both had new, white caps.

Too bad Mistress Ford didn't make shoes. Amy's toes were squeezed against the ends of the dried out ones she wore. Each step hurt. But she'd have to wait until she found somebody who wanted her and Sarah before she got something like that, or till she found a way to earn enough money herself to buy them.

If she did manage to get the money, would she rather spend it on shoes, on cloth for a gown, or on her trip back to England? What should she have first? She thought again of her aunt and uncle and their cozy home. Maybe she'd have the shoes or the gown first, though. That way she could arrive looking proper.

Every day Amy set the table when they ate and washed up after each meal. *I want to learn as much as I can,* she thought.

At first she made mistakes, like putting a greasy cooking pot in the pan of dishwater before the trenchers they ate from. But Mistress Ford kept her eye on everything, and soon Amy did an excellent job of the dishwashing.

Mistress Ford handed Amy the water bucket one day and said, "You are such a good 'elper, you may get water for me." And she allowed Amy to peel potatoes for dinner.

One day Amy got up before the rooster crowed to lay the fire in the big brick fireplace. First she took the shovel Mistress Ford used to remove the ashes and scooped them into a bucket the way she had seen Mistress Ford do it.

Mistress Ford must have heard Amy banging in the grate. Down she came from the loft with her gray hair sticking out all over. "What are you doing, child?" she asked. "That is too 'eavy for you."

"It isn't," Amy said. She lugged wood over. "I can do it. You go back to bed." After laying all those fires for Virginia while he brought them here, she knew how.

This one was easier to build than a campfire had been. If embers were left, she'd fan them to get the fire going again. A campfire always had to be done over from the beginning.

Every morning it was out cold. Each stick of wood had to be collected from the forest, as well. Here, Mistress Ford kept dry wood and tinder in a box beside the hearth. If blowing on the embers didn't ignite them, Amy could make a spark with the flint and steel and start it that way. Much simpler than how Virginia did it—rubbing sticks together.

Mistress Ford stood and watched Amy for a while and must have seen that she could in fact lay a fire, so she prepared oatmeal and cornbread for breakfast. She had everything ready to cook by the time Amy had the fire blazing.

Amy got out the coffee grinder and ground up the beans. Then she filled the pot with water and hung it on a hook in the fireplace to boil.

After breakfast, Mistress Ford took a large pot and gathered some lengths of string. She headed out the back door with them.

Amy raised her eyebrows when she saw the pot and the strings. "I'm going to make candles," Mistress Ford said. "You may 'elp."

Mistress Ford lit a fire in a ring of rocks outside the back door and set the iron pot over it. She put chunks of beef fat in the pot and stoked the fire till the fat almost simmered. Next she tied six of the strings to a metal rod and placed that across the pot with the strings hanging into the melted fat.

"You watch 'em," she said to Amy. "When the strings 'ave a goodly bit of fat stuck to 'em put the rod 'ere across the drying rack." She showed Amy how to use a folded up tea towel to grip the rod and lift it to a wooden rack next to the pot. "You must be careful the tallow doesn't drip on you. It would burn." She took a different rod with cords tied to it and placed that across the pot. "When the tallow drying on the strings starts to 'arden, put 'em back to pick up more."

Amy nodded and placed a rod across the pot. "I understand. I shall do it."

Mistress Ford watched until Amy could dip the candles correctly before she went back inside. "I shall leave the door open so I can see you," she said as she went in.

Through the open door, Amy saw Sarah still sitting in front of the fire. She scowled. *This colony is no place for uppish gentry girls.* Amy thought again how her life had changed since Father had been lost.

Mistress Ford stopped in the doorway. "Would you like me to make you some sweet biscuits?" she asked Sarah, as if she were worried about her and wanted to do something to make her feel better.

Sarah took her thumb out of her mouth and said, "Sweet biscuits? I love them. Can you make the kind with raisins?"

"Of course. I shall make oatmeal raisin biscuits. You may 'elp." Mistress Ford smiled and patted Sarah's head.

Sarah smiled back and didn't pull away this time. It was the first time Amy had seen a smile on her sister's face since they'd washed up on that shore.

Amy watched Mistress Ford mix up the dough, drop it in lumps on a baking pan, and pop that in the oven. The smell of baking sweet biscuits wafted out the door to where she worked. Ummmm—delicious.

Sarah got up. "I shall wash the bowl and spoon for you," she said to Mistress Ford.

Amy kept working on the candles without a word to Sarah about deciding to help at long last. She didn't want Sarah to change her mind.

When Amy had used up all the beef fat and had a few dozen candles hanging from the drying rack, she left them to harden and went out to Mister William's forge.

Charles stood tending the fire. He flashed a crooked, arrogant grin, his face crimson because of being so close to the furnace.

He's so vain, Amy thought. *He stands with a lofty air like he thinks he's royalty.* She decided not to look at him.

"Now you get back in the 'ouse," Mister William said. "'Tis no place for a girl out 'ere."

"Especially not a gentry girl," Charles said with his customary sneer. "Gentry girls can't do anything but sit around and sip coffee with cream."

Hah! What did he know? She could do lots of difficult things. "I can paddle a canoe and cook fish over a campfire. That's not sitting around drinking coffee."

"You can't." Charles rolled his eyes. "Don't make up lies."

"I can," Amy insisted. "And they're not lies. One day while paddling through the swamp we saw a giant cat with a short, crooked tail. It killed a bird as tall as Mistress Ford's turkeys, except the bird was skinny." She didn't think Charles had ever seen anything like that.

Charles laughed. "There's no swamp."

"I paddled in it. How could I make up something if I had not seen it? And they don't have cats that big in England. I'd never heard of one before."

Charles turned his back on her.

Amy didn't look at him either as she left for the house. *I'm not going to talk to him any more,* she thought. But she knew she'd have to, if they were to live with the same family.

The biscuits were done, and Mistress Ford gave her one. "Thank you," she said, and sat at the table across from Sarah to nibble it.

Sarah leaned closer to Amy and whispered. "I don't think she's a witch anymore, do you? These biscuits are much too good to be witch biscuits."

Amy shook her head. "You're so strange, Sarah. Nobody thinks all people who wear black are witches. She's nice."

Priscilla

The morning after the candle dipping, Amy said to her sister, "We've been in Jamestown for two weeks and still haven't found anybody who wants us. I have not thought of anything I can do to earn money, either. We can't stay in the Fords' house forever."

Sarah sprinkled maple sugar on her oatmeal and took a spoonful. "I'm going to."

But Amy knew Mistress Ford and Mister William didn't have room for two extra people. She wondered if Priscilla had it any better.

"Will you take us to call on Priscilla?" Amy asked Mistress Ford. "We haven't seen where she's living."

"Of course, child," Mistress Ford said. "I'm sure she's doing fine. Today is market day. I shall take you to town with me."

So Amy and Sarah donned their caps, and with Mistress Ford carrying her basket, the three of them walked to the village square. In the open area, where the town meeting had been held, vendors had set up booths to sell things they'd grown or made. Amy saw baskets of apples and pears for sale. The man called Josiah, who she'd seen the day she arrived, tended a pen with six chickens clucking and pecking at the ground. He nodded to her and she returned the nod. Next to Josiah, an Indian sat with a few fish laid on a cloth spread on the ground. Amy took a good look at the Indian to make sure it was not Virginia. But he had a lined face and hair sprinkled with gray. Someone older. Coming up the street toward her, four geese trotted in a line. A skinny, flustered-looking boy with yellow hair hanging in his eyes waved a switch over them. Two brown dogs, tied to a tree, barked at the geese. Amy laughed.

She wondered if she should check to see if anyone had shoes to sell. But what could she buy them with? She'd look in on Priscilla.

"I'll show you the shop where your friend works," Mistress Ford said. "'Tis around the next corner 'ere." She pointed. "When you're done visiting, come back to the market and find me."

Amy nodded. "I remember seeing that sign the day we went to the meeting."

She and Sarah set off for the shop. "Jamestown is small when compared to English cities," Amy said, "but it's nice to have houses and places where people work, instead of only trees and muck."

Sarah nodded and plodded along beside her.

Amy and Sarah walked on a road packed firm by hundreds of feet, much better for walking than the forest had been. Amy knocked at the door of the shop with the needle and thread sign.

A bell tinkled when Priscilla opened it. She wore a new, dark blue frock with a lacy white collar and stood with a wide, wide smile.

"Oh...you've got a new gown!" Amy exclaimed, first thing, even before she said hello. "You're fortunate."

"Aye. Mistress Charity made it for me. You know what my other one looked like."

Like mine, Amy thought, grimacing and looking down at her faded and worn smock.

"People in a sewing shop can't wear worn-out clothes. Come in." Priscilla stepped aside and looked the other way while Amy and Sarah entered.

"I shall make us tea," Priscilla said. She led them into a room behind the shop. "'Tis a new drink. Mistress Moody, the lady from the store, gave some to Mistress Charity when she picked up the new gown she'd had made." Priscilla smiled again. "I'm so glad you came to call." She looked as contented as a cat curled in front of the fire.

Amy sat on the bench Priscilla showed her to. "We drink coffee at the Fords' house." She sniffed the tea.

"Do you like it here in the colony?" Sarah asked.

"I do. 'Tis a wonderful place to wait for Mother."

Priscilla served the tea and a few biscuits she found. "Mistress Charity is off to the market," she said, setting cups on the table.

The whole time she ate the biscuits and drank the tea, Amy felt shabby next to her friend. *It looks as if I am the lower class girl now and Priscilla the gentry one,* Amy thought.

After the tea, Priscilla showed them her tiny room opening off the shop—her own private room. She didn't sleep on the floor in front of the fireplace as Amy and Sarah did.

"I 'ave never 'ad a room of my own before," Priscilla said. "I 'ave always 'ad only a corner of a big room."

Amy felt she had been pampered. "I've always had my own room," she said.

"I'm so glad I came to the New Land. I shall never go back to London, not even for a visit," said Priscilla.

Sarah nodded. "I will never get on a ship."

Amy ignored her sister. "Your mother will be found just as they will find my father." She brushed her hair back from her forehead. "Sarah and I can't stay here without a family, though. We must go back to London and wait. I still haven't written to Edmund. Perhaps I won't. I want to have something good to say to him when I do. Right now all I have to tell him is that Father is still missing. If I wait till we get back to England, I can see Edmund himself and explain."

Priscilla shook her head. "'Tis better in the New Land, much, much better. I shall wait 'ere."

Amy wished she knew how to do something that would make somebody want her, the way Mistress Charity wanted Priscilla. Nobody in the whole colony wanted Amy and Sarah—nobody. Gentry girls were useless.

"It is a blessing you can sew," Amy said. It wasn't her fault the ship sank. It wasn't her fault they didn't have a mother or father. She also realized it wasn't her fault she had been raised wealthy and didn't know how to do anything useful. Perhaps Mistress Ford felt she and Sarah were a burden. Mistress Ford wasn't able to do a lot of the things she could before. Having Amy and Sarah in the house made a lot of extra work. *I don't want to be a burden*, Amy thought.

When she'd finished her second cup of tea, Amy thanked her friend and went off to find Mistress Ford.

On Sunday, wearing her old and tattered gown, she went to church with Mister and Mistress Ford, Sarah, and Charles.

Some people stared and shook their heads. Amy assumed it was because she and Sarah looked so shabby, but most people smiled. Charles strutted in a shirt with a fancy collar and laughed at Amy and Sarah. All five of them sat together.

After church, since it was the day Priscilla did not have to work, Amy walked with Sarah to visit her again.

Charles didn't have to work on Sunday, either. So when Amy and Sarah went to town, he went with them. Amy wasn't sure she liked his company—he was so nasty. But she didn't want to tell him he couldn't join them. That would make her as ill-mannered as he was.

On the way to Mistress Charity's tailoring shop, Amy and Sarah both took a look at the shore. "After I check for an English ship, I have to see if Virginia has come to visit," Amy said.

Sarah nodded. "Me, too."

But Virginia wasn't with the Indian traders camped on the beach.

"What do you girls do all day in that sewing shop?" Charles asked.

"We talk to each other," Amy said.

"And drink tea," said Sarah.

Charles teased them. "You're trying to act like fine ladies when you aren't."

Amy tried to politely disregard him. "We play checkers, too," she said. "Mistress Charity has a checkers set."

"Do you ever win?"

"Of course," Amy said. "Different people do."

"Sometimes I win," said Sarah.

Charles laughed. "Your little sister beats you? Aren't you ashamed?"

Amy thought she'd better not say anything after that remark. For sure, if she did, it would be rude.

"I'll play you sometime," Charles said. "I'll beat you, too. I'm good at checkers. I'm the best in the world."

Amy clamped her jaw together so she wouldn't say something unladylike about Charles and his bragging.

But Sarah spoke up. "Amy's good at lots of things. I am, too. When we traveled up here, Amy paddled the canoe and I helped cut brush."

"Another one of those made-up stories like the one about the giant cat," Charles said. He laughed.

"That's not a made-up story," said Sarah, although she couldn't have known for sure which cat Amy had told him about. "We saw lots of cats—and bears and raccoons and rabbits and snakes."

"You're a liar like your sister. A savage would not allow a girl to paddle his canoe. I'm sure he was glad to be rid of you two nuisances when he got here."

He thinks he's the only person in the whole world who can do anything, Amy thought. She walked along in silence. At last the three of them arrived at the town square. Charles left the girls there and swaggered off to find his friends. Amy was sure they were as vain as he was.

They probably sit around and brag to each other all day long, she thought.

At Mistress Charity's shop, Priscilla put on the kettle for chocolate this time and got out sweet biscuits.

"I 'ave presents for both of you," Priscilla said, even before she mixed the chocolate. "I 'ave been practicing 'ow to sew a skirt so I can learn to make a gown, and I 'ave made you aprons."

She ran to a chest and returned with two sparkling-white aprons. "I 'ope they fit. I made a medium one and a small one. I 'ad to guess. Try 'em on."

Amy and Sarah put on the new aprons over their tattered gowns. "They're perfect," Amy said. "Thank you."

"Perfect," Sarah echoed. "Oh, it's almost as good as getting a new gown." She flung her arms around Priscilla's neck.

"They make our old gowns look so much better." Amy gave her friend a hug, too.

Priscilla smiled so wide it looked as if her face would split.

Of course Amy and Sarah left the aprons on while they drank the chocolate. "I may never take it off," Amy said.

"I shall," said Sarah. "I'll take it off to sleep so it won't get wrinkly."

Now that Amy had a new apron, she didn't feel so scruffy beside Priscilla in her stylish gown. "The store still has no fabric for gowns," Amy said with a long face. "Ships have come in since we've been here, but all they have on them are things like coffee, chocolate, spices, china, windows for houses, iron to make tools out of, not ever any cloth for gowns."

"We'll never get any," Sarah said.

Amy was ready to agree with her sister, this time. It had been so long.

Priscilla changed the subject to one that was not so dismal. "Let's do a reading lesson today instead of playing checkers. Let's do spelling." She got out a slate.

Amy was pleased with the suggestion. It took her mind off the no fabric problem. "Today is the Lord's Day, so we must read nothing but the Bible. But I suppose 'tis all right to spell Bible words."

Sarah went to talk to Mistress Charity.

Amy said the words and Priscilla wrote them.

"New," said Amy, "for New Testament."

N-o-o, Priscilla wrote.

Amy fixed it for her.

Priscilla looked at her slate. "'ow can e-w spell 'oo'?"

"I don't know," Amy said. "Remember it like I do. Next word—old."

Priscilla wrote the word correctly this time. "That one makes sense," she said, and nodded.

Amy laughed. "Lots of spelling doesn't make sense." She shrugged.

Priscilla looked at the two words she had written and her face broke into a wide smile. "You know, I had a glorious idea. I don't know why I didn't think of it before. I 'ave been wondering 'ow I can pay for the reading lessons. Why don't I make the new gowns for you and Sarah to pay for 'em?"

"Except we don't have anything to make them out of," Amy reminded her.

"Aye. But we will. A ship will come in with something soon. You'll see. Mistress Charity wants me to learn 'ow to make an 'ole gown by myself, and I can practice on you and Sarah. The biggest thing I 'ave ever made is those aprons." Priscilla beamed at her friend.

Amy smiled back. "I'd love to have you make it. I don't even care what it looks like or what color it is or anything, so long as it's new." Then she realized that sounded impolite and said, "I don't mean you would do a bad job. I mean I'm anxious for a new gown."

"I know. That's all right," Priscilla said. "Mistress Charity says I sew neat tiny stitches. 'Twill be good."

Amy and Priscilla practiced spelling until Amy and Sarah had to leave. "Thank you again for the aprons and for that wonderful idea for getting new gowns," Amy said as she left.

Now all they needed was a ship to come in with the right cargo. One would come soon, maybe tomorrow. She was hopeful again.

When Amy and Sarah arrived back at the Fords', Charles stood by the table holding four fish strung together on a vine.

"Look what Charles has for us," said Mistress Ford, "nice fresh fish."

Oh no. It reminded Amy of her trip through the swamp. She puckered her nose as if she smelled something that had been rotten for six weeks. Sarah did, too.

"Don't you like fish?" Mistress Ford asked.

"I do," Amy said. "But I ate it most every day while we traveled up here. I don't want to taste it ever again."

Charles rolled his eyes. "Now you're going to tell us you can catch fish, too."

"Virginia caught them," Sarah said.

"Our Indian friend," said Amy, when Charles still looked like he didn't believe it.

Amy and Sarah left him with his expression of disbelief and went off to do their before dinner chores. Both of them ate fish for evening meal, even though, for Amy, eating it brought back unpleasant memories.

Amy's Job

The next day Amy leaned on a table out in the forge while Mister William and Charles hammered away on fancy hinges for somebody's kitchen cupboards.

"Now you stay out of the way, Amy," Mister William warned. "I don't want you to get burned by sparks from the fire or 'ave something 'eavy fall on you."

"I won't get in the way," Amy said. "I want something different to do, that's all. I like keeping house, but I wish I had a book to read."

"You can read?" Mister William paused in his work and raised his eyebrows.

"I've never heard of a girl who could read before," Charles said, sneering.

"Of course I can," said Amy. "I had a tutor when I was in England. My father thought all girls should be able to. Sarah can, too."

"No. Girls can't do anything." Charles kept hammering on the hinge. "Not one as little as Sarah, anyway. Why would anyone waste time teaching something to a girl?"

Amy glared at him.

112

"Now, maybe she can," Mister William cut in. "Girls in England can sometimes read, if they're gentry girls and don't 'ave to work to s'port the family. I 'ave 'eard of it."

Charles continued to scowl and looked doubtful.

Amy scowled right back. "Well, I can," she said, trying to muster up as much arrogance as he had. "Boys don't think girls can do anything. I shall find something to read to you and prove it." She ran off to the house, letting the door bang as she went in.

"Don't slam the door," Mistress Ford said.

"Sorry, ma'am. What have you got that I can read? I want to prove to Charles that I am able to."

Mistress Ford stopped cutting up the carrots she'd been slicing for the stew. "You can read?" she asked, the same as Mister William had.

Amy nodded. "What do you have?"

"The Bible." Mistress Ford put down the carrots and her knife, wiped her hands on her apron, and went to fetch it.

She came back with a leather-bound book, thick and heavy. Amy had seen it before when Mister William read to them on Sunday evenings. Mistress Ford put the Bible on the table beside the carrots and opened the fancy brass hasp that kept it closed. She turned to Genesis.

"Read that," she said, pointing to verse one.

"In the beginning God created the heavens and the earth," Amy read.

"Wait a minute. I'll get somethin' else. You could 'ave memorized that from when you went to meeting." Mistress Ford turned a lot of pages to the Book of Joshua. "There. Read that."

Amy read: "Now after the death of Moses, the servant of the Lord, it came to pass…"

Mistress Ford leaned over the Bible, her mouth moving silently with Amy's as Amy read. "'Tis enough. You really are reading. I never would 'ave guessed a girl could read. 'Course you come from fine folks. I s'pose there wasn't much else for you to do in that sort of a family. You must 'ave 'ad all kinds of servants."

Sarah came from where she sat by the fire with her thumb in her mouth. She took the thumb out. "I can read, too," she said.

"Show me."

Sarah opened the Bible to another chapter and read a verse for Mistress Ford. "See?" she said.

Mistress Ford shook her head. "And you such a wee thing."

"Well, if you can read," she said to Amy, as she went back to her carrots, "you can teach others. We shall start a school for girls. We need one 'ere. There isn't one. Only one for boys."

She looked at Sarah. "You're a bit young—to teach others, I mean—but p'rhaps you can 'elp your sister."

Amy brightened at Mistress Ford's suggestion. It sounded daring, starting a school. She'd teach girls to read and write. Father had often said how accomplished she was at penmanship.

Then she realized, people paid money to have someone teach them. Maybe her problems were solved. She'd save the money she got from teaching girls to read and use it to pay for her trip back to England. Every day she remembered her Aunt Elizabeth and Uncle Edward with their safe, warm home. She smiled. *I guess gentry girls aren't useless after all*, she thought.

"May I take the Bible to the forge and read for Mister William and Charles?" she asked.

"I don't want you to take it out where they have sparks from that fire. Run and tell them to come in."

Amy tore out the door with Sarah at her heels. "Come and listen to me," she said to Mister William and Charles. "I shall read the Bible. Mistress Ford won't let me bring it out here."

"It feels like time for a cup of coffee, anyway," Mister William said. He and Charles laid down their tools and followed Amy inside.

When everyone had seated themselves at the table, Amy opened the Bible to yet a different passage, this one in the middle of Chronicles. "David made houses in the city of David and prepared a place for the ark...," Amy read.

Mister William interrupted. "'Tis true. She can read."

"I've never met a girl who could read before," Charles said for the third time. "I can. A little bit. Names, if they're people I know, but that's all. I've never wanted to read anything else." He shrugged.

Amy was amazed. This was something different. Charles, who considered himself the best at everything, couldn't read. "You believe I can do something you can't?" she asked, unable to let this opportunity slip by without saying something.

"I've just heard you. But why do you want to read? My mother tried to make me do it. It's a waste of time, I think."

"I love reading," Amy said.

"So do I," said Sarah.

"You can read, too?" Charles raised both eyebrows at Sarah. "Reading is for sissies. Girls can't do anything else, so they may as well read."

Mistress Ford interrupted. "I think Amy should start a school and teach other girls to read. She'd charge money, of course."

"'Old on a minute there," Mister William said, a sliver of wood dangling from between his teeth. "That's a pretty outlandish idea you've come up with. Girls don't need to go to school. Why should a girl know how to read?"

"To read the Bible, of course. We came to this New Land to get away from old ideas in England. Now you want to bring those ideas 'ere."

Mister William leaned back and gaped at her. "Well...I don't know now. That's never been done before that I ever 'eard of. A school for girls?" He shook his head.

"There aren't any 'ere. We shall 'ave the first one. Right in front of our own fireplace. Reading lessons for girls." Mistress Ford wiped her hands on her apron. "'Tis a New Land we 'ave come to. We're going to do new things." She nodded as if that settled the matter. "Right now is the perfect time of year for lessons, too. Nobody can grow things, 'tis winter. There'll be plenty of girls to teach. In summertime children work on family farms."

Mister William looked doubtful. "We can try it, I s'pose. See if anyone wants to send their girls. 'Tis my guess they won't." He got up to get himself a cup of coffee.

"I'll teach you, too," Amy said to Charles.

He put his hand up as if pushing her back. "I don't need to know how to read. Reading is for sissies."

And smart people, Amy thought. She was delighted with the idea of giving lessons and couldn't wait to say something to Priscilla. Priscilla could come and be her first pupil. "May I go over and tell Priscilla?" Amy asked.

"Yes, child. Run and tell your friend. Put on that shawl I always wear. 'Tis getting cold out these days. I'd better knit you one. I 'ave yarn left from last year's shearing."

Sarah went with her. They ran the whole way, which made Amy's feet in her too tight shoes ache a lot. "The first thing I'm going to buy when someone pays me to teach them, is a new pair of shoes," she said as she raced along.

When Priscilla heard the idea of the school, she exclaimed, "I can come and learn to read better! I shall pay you with what I earn sewing."

"You don't need to pay. We're friends."

Mistress Charity smiled at the three of them. "All girls should know how to read," she said. "Some don't think so, but I do. I have a book you can use." She got up to get it. It was an old book of poetry.

Amy reached for the book, feeling stunned. Books. How could she give lessons without books? And where would she get them? Her excitement and her thoughts of earning money by teaching reading wafted away like smoke up the chimney.

14 A Ship

The instant she got back to the Fords', Amy asked, "Where will I get books for the school?" She felt like crying.

"I never thought of that," Mistress Ford said. She looked up from the bread she was kneading. "You should 'ave an 'Orn Book for the alphabet and a 'rithmetic book. We'll ask the church to get donations. Churches are good at that sort of thing. Lots of folks 'ave books in their homes that nobody ever reads. Perhaps they would give them to us."

So Amy made a notice on a piece of paper that something had been wrapped in to put up on the board at the church. She and Mistress Ford went down and tacked it there first chance they got.

The notice said: "School For Girls—and others if they wish to attend. Please donate books for the girls to use. Put them here." An arrow pointed to a box that Charles had made.

In two days a big pile of books had collected for Amy's school. Mister William and Charles went down with the wheelbarrow to tote them home. There were story books, poetry books, history books, and the very important Horn Book to teach reading.

"These books are taking up a lot of space in the 'ouse," Mister William said as he dumped more inside the door. "I'll build a shed out back to keep them in."

"Maybe you could make a school room for Amy, by the forge," Mistress Ford suggested.

Mister William chewed on his sliver of wood. "We'll wait and see if this school idea catches on, see if people keep sending their girls."

"Don't wait too long. There isn't a lot of space in 'ere."

In no time Amy had six girls to teach. Mister William shook his head in amazement. All of the girls brought a penny each week. Amy saved the pennies in an old jam crock. Soon she'd have enough for those shoes she needed.

The church collected more and more books. Now Amy had five slates, too. "I'd better make that new schoolhouse," Mister William said at suppertime one day.

The fathers of the students came over Saturday afternoons, and any other time they had a few spare minutes, to help build it. They brought their own hammers and saws. In no time the schoolhouse looked like a real building. The only parts left to do were the windows and the fireplace. Amy walked to the shore each afternoon to look for a ship that might have windows.

In the meantime, Amy taught the girls on the floor in front of the Fords' fireplace.

She wore her old gown while she taught. Would she never get a new one? As soon as she was able to buy the stuff, Priscilla would make it. Nothing had come in on the last ship, however, and still no news of the *Hope*.

Two days later, as Amy finished drying the last trencher from the midday meal, she saw Priscilla racing along the street.

"Amy! Amy!" Priscilla yelled. "A ship. Look!"

Amy dashed out front and sure enough, a ship with white sails billowing in the breeze sailed closer and closer to the colony. "I must ask them for news of Father." Amy darted back inside and flung her tea towel onto a peg. "Surely this one will have cloth."

She took Priscilla's hand and the two of them dashed to the shore.

Since it was Saturday afternoon, and school was only a half day on Saturdays, Amy could wait as long as needed. She and Priscilla sat on a barrel lying on the beach ready to be loaded onto the ship when at last it offloaded its cargo. She smelled tobacco in the barrel right through the wood. All of the barrels weren't full of tobacco. Some were marked cornmeal or flour. Stacks of lumber waited on the beach to be loaded as well.

Three men with black skin unloaded a wagon of more barrels. Amy knew the biggest man, the one with his hair shaved off to the skin. He was Moses, and worked for Mister Moody at the store. She'd seen him many times on her trips to town. He was the first man she had ever seen with skin that color. Like with Virginia, nobody could pronounce Moses's African name when he arrived in the colony. The people had to give him a new one.

She glanced over where men worked to build a better dock so all ships could tie up, the same as they did in England. Most ships still anchored off shore and the sailors rowed in with the goods.

After the merchants sold the tobacco, lumber, cornmeal, or flour to somebody in England, the ships brought back luxury items that people in the colony did not have. Amy hoped that this trip they brought dress goods, not silverware, chocolate, or spices.

She glanced the other way, along the water's edge where a group of Indians had beached their canoes and were trading with the townsfolk. Sarah stood by them talking to three boys who had been left with the boats.

She's most likely trying to talk them into giving her a canoe, Amy thought, smiling. She had gotten tired of listening to Sarah say she wanted a canoe like Virginia's. Whatever did Sarah need a canoe for? They couldn't sail that across the ocean to England. She'd noticed the Indians who came to the colony could speak a lot more English than Virginia.

Charles was over trading with them as well. But Amy stayed put, even though one of them might have been Virginia. If he were there, she trusted Sarah to bring him to her. News of Father was more important.

It seemed to be taking longer than usual for the ship to come in. At last the sailors put a boat over the side and unloaded cargo to row it to shore—things in boxes and barrels like the one Amy sat on. Any one of them could hold dress goods.

She groaned. "We shall never be able to tell by looking at the outside," she said. "Many different things might be within."

She waited at the water's edge and asked the sailors as they rowed to shore, "Have you seen a shipwrecked man named Solomon Purdy? Have you heard of a storm-wrecked ship called the *Hope*?"

Every sailor shook his head and replied that he hadn't. Amy began to think maybe the mystery would never be solved.

Then her high hopes took over, and she thought surely he had made it back to England. Soon she would hear from Aunt Elizabeth. Possibly this ship had a letter.

Lots of people waited to see what the ship brought.

"There's Mister Moody from the store," Priscilla said. "Let's ask him if he's expecting cloth."

Amy and Priscilla made their way through the crowd of onlookers and waiting barrels to Mister Moody. He stood with his hands full of lists.

"Good day, Mister Moody," Amy said. "It is a very nice day today, is it not?" You always had to say something pleasant first. Her mother had taught her that.

Priscilla poked her in the ribs. "Ask," she said, low enough that Mister Moody wouldn't hear.

Amy continued. "Pardon me for asking, sir, but are you expecting any stuff to make gowns?"

He shuffled through his lists, got to the end of the stack and went back a few. "Yes," he said. "I should have linen and wool both coming in. We'll have to wait and see if they do." He smiled down at Amy and Priscilla.

They smiled up at him. "Oh good. May we be first to choose?" Amy asked.

"You are here first. So I guess you may. They don't always bring what people ask for, though."

Amy knew that. She'd been waiting for the cloth for weeks. It took the rest of the afternoon to unload the ship. Amy stood impatiently on the sand while each little boat got rowed to shore and whatever it carried was sorted into piles for the receiving merchant. Mister Moody had the largest stack. He had the biggest dry goods business.

He made a check on one of his lists as Moses added each box or barrel to his heap. Finally he said to Amy. "The wool came in, but the linen did not. It's in that barrel." He pointed with his pencil.

The girls clutched each other and jumped up and down, getting sand stuck to their shoes. "When may I see it? When will you get it to your store?" Amy didn't care whether her new gown was wool or linen, so long as she got one.

"Come Monday. It should be ready by then."

"Let's go measure you," Priscilla said.

They ran the whole way. When they arrived at Mistress Charity's, Priscilla fetched a tape to measure Amy, how tall she was, around her, and the length of her arms. They needed to know Sarah's measurements, too, so Amy raced to the Fords'.

As she dashed past the beach, she noticed the Indian traders had left. Back at the Fords', Mistress Ford paced in front of the fireplace wiping her hands on her apron.

Mister William knocked out one pipe on a brick in the chimney corner and filled another, looking as agitated as his wife. Charles sat at the table and drummed his fingers.

"They'll bring 'er back." Mister William drew on his pipe as he held a flaming sliver to it.

"Who'll bring who back?" Amy asked. "What happened?"

Mistress Ford wiped her hands on her apron again and said, "Sarah. Charles saw her go off with those savages."

"Was one of them Virginia?" asked Amy. "Sarah might want to go with him." If Virginia had visited, and Sarah hadn't told her, Amy would be angry.

Charles shook his head. "I don't know. She wanted them to give her a canoe. I heard her say she'd trade something."

"Did Sarah look distressed?" Mistress Ford asked Charles.

"I didn't notice," Charles said and shrugged.

How could Sarah leave her in the colony by herself with no friends? Sarah was her sister. Sisters were supposed to stick together. She sat down hard on a bench. "Sarah has no sense."

Mistress Ford continued to pace. "We have to get Sarah back. Go after her, William. Take the gun."

"I'll get Moody and Anderson the carpenter and a few of the others." He took his hat and left.

"How do they know what tribe the Indians are? How will they know where to find them?" Charles asked. "All savages look alike to me."

"We don't know. All we can do is guess." Mistress Ford continued to wipe her hands with such energy Amy feared she would wear a hole clear through the apron.

Mister William didn't get back from talking to the neighbors till the sun was sinking in a blaze of orange behind the far ridge of hills. "We're going at first light," he said.

Mistress Ford nodded. "That's wise. 'Twill be dark soon. No sense 'aving you men go missing, too." She still wiped her hands at least once every minute.

Mister William hung his hat on a hook and sat at the table across from Charles. "I 'ave five men to go with me: Moody, Anderson, that new apprentice who's working for Moody, Moses, and a fellow from the lumberyard. Is supper ready?"

"Dear me. I forgot all about it." Mistress Ford hustled to the pantry.

While a few ears of corn boiled in the pot hanging in the fireplace, she mixed up biscuits. She found a cold ham in the larder as well.

Amy ate her supper in silence, feeling annoyed with her sister.

Charles gulped down half a biscuit at once and said, "Perhaps Sarah has been kidnapped. Maybe they weren't savages she knew."

Amy choked on a piece of ham. What if Charles were right? What if Sarah had been taken against her will and the Indians, at this moment, were cutting off her hair and the skin it grew out of? Virginia was a good Indian, but that didn't mean all of them were. Amy couldn't eat. She had been angry at her sister.

With Sarah gone missing, Amy tossed and turned the whole night long. She had gotten used to cuddling with Sarah. She had never thought she could fret this way about her, but Sarah was all she had right now. Would she ever see her again?

Amy rose before first light and gulped down her morning meal.

Charles finished first, though. He put on his coat and took his fur cap and his gun. "I'm ready."

"Don't you get trigger 'appy now," Mister William said. "We don't want to shoot somebody by accident. 'Tisn't a war party. The guns are in case we need protection. We might run into bears." He reached for the door. "We'll skip church this morning, 'Attie. Getting Sarah back is more important."

Mistress Ford nodded. "I shall go. I'll ask everyone to pray for Sarah."

Amy went to the river with Mister William and Charles. "Can I go with you?" she asked, as she hurried to keep up with their long legs. "I'm used to talking to Indians. I'm good in the forest."

"No," Mister William said. "There may be shooting. You stay 'ome and pray." He set his mouth in a grim line.

The other men, except for Anderson, were waiting on shore when Amy arrived with Mister William and Charles. Two men Amy didn't know were coming waited with them. Mister William put his gun in the skiff with Moody's gun. Amy waited anxiously for Anderson. He galloped up on a black horse and hitched it to a post.

"Should we go north or south? Did anybody see which way they went?" Anderson asked.

Everyone looked at Charles. "I didn't," Charles said. "I didn't pay any attention." He shrugged.

"We shall go north." Mister William pointed in that direction. "Most savages who come 'ere to trade come from there."

Mister Moody, Mister William, Charles, and Mister Anderson rowed out to where a sailing ketch floated at anchor. They all got into it. The skiff they tied to the buoy that had moored the ketch. The other five men followed in another boat. As soon as they got the first sail up and turned northward, two large Indian canoes glided silently around the point into view.

"Look," Amy shouted, not knowing if the men were too far off to hear her or not. "Mister William, look!"

Mister William and the others furled their sails and waited for the Indians to come alongside. The men held their guns at the ready.

Amy squinted into the distance. The sun was just now rising high enough to give light to see. Was it a war party? Amy looked for spears. Where was Sarah?

Visitors

When the canoes got close, Amy could make out the people.

Charles shouted, "Sarah is in the second one."

A band of copper disks around Sarah's forehead gleamed in the morning sunshine like brand-new pennies. She sat between two Indian boys who were decked out in body paint, shells, trinkets, and beaming from ear to ear. Two rows of circles, alternating blue and red, had been painted across Sarah's cheeks. Three blue lines went from her bottom lip over her chin. Strands of bright beads, or perhaps painted seeds, dangled about her neck. She waved to her sister and to the men in the boats.

Amy's mouth fell open. Sarah looked happy! Amy remembered Sarah had hidden behind her the first time she had encountered an Indian. And for many days she would not sit beside Virginia nor let him touch her, even when taking the food he passed. *For certain her attitude toward Indians has changed*, Amy thought. All of the people in the canoes looked as if they were having a wonderful time. These Indians must not be ones who cut off the hair of English people and killed them.

The Indians and the Englishmen sailed to shore and beached their crafts. Sarah climbed out and shook hands with every one of the braves she traveled with, still grinning.

"Why'd you go with them?" Amy demanded.

"I wanted them to give me a canoe," Sarah said. "I didn't know they'd keep me till next morning. I thought I'd be back for supper."

"We worried about you."

Sarah stopped smiling. "I'm sorry. But once I got to their village, I couldn't come home by myself. I didn't have my own boat. I had to wait for them to bring me."

"Did they give you a canoe?"

"No. But they gave me these beads and this." She held out a furry squirrel stuffed with something and made into a toy. "Now I have to get them a book. To trade. We roasted an animal called a 'possum for evening meal."

Sarah ran off. Amy and the village men watched her go.

"She shouldn't 'ave done that," Mister William said. "We all worried."

"She's lucky," said Charles. "I wish I could go to an Indian camp. I want one of those copper disk headbands."

Amy shook her head.

Sarah returned with the book in a flash. Mistress Ford hustled along behind, dressed for church. Sarah had brought a book from Amy's school collection, nursery rhymes that someone had given them. "It's got pictures," Sarah said. "They won't be able to read the words."

She handed the book to an Indian with deep creases going from his nose to the corners of his mouth. His forehead had three of those lines Father had said a person got from thinking a lot. He stood on shore with his head held high like someone important. More paint adorned his face than the others', and shiny shells dangled from his earlobes. He also had wicked looking spears and a dagger.

"This is Owasowas," Sarah said to introduce him. "He's the chief."

"'Tank you," Owasowas said, taking the book.

"I taught him how to say that," said Sarah.

The group on the beach waited, with Sarah waving, while Owasowas and the others got into the canoes and began paddling back to their village.

Amy watched until they were out of sight around the point. The whole time, Owasowas held the book tight against his chest.

"Well, I'll be," Mister William said. "I've never seen anything like that."

Mister Moody nodded. "I haven't, either."

Mistress Ford didn't scold Sarah for staying away over night. Amy figured she must be glad Sarah didn't get murdered.

The little group of Englishmen went back about their business. Amy, Sarah, Charles, and the Fords walked home. Because church was over by now, all of them missed it this week.

After lessons on Monday, Amy took the pennies she had earned and she and Sarah dashed to the store to get the fabric. "Where is it?" Amy asked.

"Your friend picked it up. She paid for it as well."

Amy and Sarah raced to Mistress Charity's gown-making shop and rapped eagerly on the door.

Priscilla called, "Come in." She sat working on a length of pretty chestnut-colored material.

"Is that to be my new gown?" Amy asked.

"Yes." Priscilla pointed to some green stuff in a pile. "And that's for Sarah's."

Amy thought it would be the most beautiful gown she had ever owned. She knew the chestnut color would look lovely with her light hair. Getting the gown first instead of returning to England had been a good idea. The next pennies she saved she'd use to pay her passage back—after she bought shoes, of course.

"I owe money," Amy said.

"Give it to Mistress Charity," said Priscilla. "She paid."

Amy reached for the little deerskin pocket Mistress Ford had given her to keep coins in. Her linen pocket had been ruined on her trek through the swamp. It had come apart and floated away when she'd jumped into the water to save Sarah. She counted pennies out in a pile to pay Mistress Charity. Exactly sixteen pennies remained. "It will take me more than a year to save for our passage," she said, feeling glum.

Priscilla nodded. "Everything 'ere is more costly than in England."

"How long will it take to make a gown?" Amy asked. She had no idea because she couldn't sew things like that, and she'd never paid attention when Mother's seamstress sewed for her in England. She hoped it wouldn't be as long as it would take her to save for the voyage.

"A week perhaps," Priscilla answered, "maybe more. I'm slower than Miss Charity and I'm doing my best."

"Come, Sarah," Amy said, tugging on her sister's hand. "We must go so Priscilla can finish. I can't believe I'm so excited about one new thing to wear. In England I had a whole room full of gowns, all colors and all kinds. Now I'm delighted to get just one."

Sarah nodded. "I am, too."

But Amy was excited. This gown was special. She had worked for it herself.

While waiting for the gowns to be finished, Amy fell back into her school routine. Sarah took over many of the household chores Amy used to do, like washing dishes and sweeping the floor. She also helped with laundering the clothes.

"I'm glad we have the school," Sarah said to Amy at suppertime one day. "It's something useful to do. I like to be useful."

Amy stifled her urge to say she'd been trying to tell Sarah that all along. Sometimes, when Amy taught her students, Sarah sat on the floor in her new green gown and helped the girls write their letters.

"No, Esther," Sarah corrected the little girl. "Don't write your name r-e-h-t-s-E. Start over here on the other side of the slate." Sarah showed Esther how.

The brown chickens Mistress Ford kept in the backyard got to be Sarah's responsibility, too, but not the cow. Mistress Ford still milked her.

Sarah made pets of the chickens. "I love feeding them," she told Amy. "And I like gathering their eggs every morning. I have given each of the hens a name. I named them after people in the stories I heard when I lived in England." One morning when she put her basket of eggs on the table, she pointed to a brown one on top. "That one is King Arthur's," Sarah said.

"You have given a girl chicken a boy's name," Amy pointed out.

"I don't care," said Sarah, "and neither does she. She struts around like she thinks she's the king. I've named one of the turkeys, too, the one who chases me and pecks at my ankles when I go out for eggs. I call him Rascal."

Amy asked, "Why do the other turkeys not have names?"

"Because we're going to eat them. I don't want to eat something that has a name. Except I would enjoy eating Rascal."

"But you named all the chickens."

"We're not going to eat them. They're for eggs."

Amy rolled her eyes. She hadn't seen Sarah's thumb in her mouth for days now, and most of the time Sarah smiled. She must be getting used to the colony.

Mistress Ford sat knitting. "I do not have so much housework to do now," she said, "what with you girls doing it all. I shall knit a warm shawl for each of you to keep off the icy winter winds." Since Sarah had gone off with the Indians, and given everyone a good scare, Mistress Ford seemed a lot more concerned about both girls.

"It's not as cold here as it is in England," Amy said when her shawl was finished. She wrapped it around her shoulders to try it. "But it is cool enough for shawls. I'm thankful to get one."

"I shall teach you to knit, Sarah," Mistress Ford said. "'Twill keep your thumb out of your mouth."

So after supper every evening, Sarah sat in Mistress Ford's rocker and knitted on a muff to keep her hands warm.

Mistress Ford beamed at Sarah. "As soon as you're done, I shall show you 'ow to make a nice fringe on your shawl."

"I shall knit you a muff, too," Sarah said to Amy, who sat on the floor playing checkers with Charles.

"Very well," said Amy. She leaned back against the fireplace and smiled. She had beaten Charles at checkers for the sixth time in a row.

"You're getting good at checkers," Charles admitted.

"I always was," Amy said.

Sarah hadn't beaten him yet, though.

The days progressed to the middle of December and Amy's schoolhouse was finished enough that the girls could have lessons in it instead of in front of Mistress Ford's hearth. It had windows, but still no furniture. Amy had to sit on the floor with her students, but Mister William had made a big fireplace to keep the room warm. Charles cut and hauled in a huge stack of logs.

While Amy helped Sarah with the washing up from the midday meal on Saturday, a hesitant tap-tap-tap sounded at the door. Mister William, who sat finishing his coffee, got up. A stranger stood outside. Nevertheless, Mister William invited him in and ushered him to a bench at the table.

The man remained standing and fiddled with the knit cap he had plucked from his head. "Good afternoon," he said. "I'm Gideon Gilroy from the ship *Explorer*." He gestured toward the shore.

"William Ford." He shook Gideon Gilroy's hand.

"'Tis a lovely day today to be sure," the sailor continued.

"'Tis," Mistress Ford agreed, coming from the cupboard where she had been putting dishes away as Amy dried them.

The man nodded toward Amy and Sarah. "'Tis those girls I must speak with," he said. "I have news of the *Hope*. One of our crew knows of their search."

Amy flung her towel on the table. "It has been found? Is my father safe?"

"It 'as been found," he said. "My ship put in to a shore south of 'ere, to fill our water casks at a creek. 'Twas in the land claimed by Spain, so 'twas necessary to post guards..."

"My father, have you found him?" Amy interrupted, her heart pounding. She gasped for breath.

"Let the man speak," said Mister Ford.

Gideon Gilroy continued. "John and me were ordered to the top of the dune to keep watch for Spanish soldiers. I saw a vessel tossed over that dune and partway down t'other side. 'Twas a great storm for sure that threw a ship so far."

Amy nodded. She had been in such a great storm.

"Me and John, we made our way to the ship and we saw her name. 'Twas the *Hope*. She lay in three pieces on the sand, one part of 'er in the creek."

"But the people. What happened to her passengers and crew?"

"We saw no people. With a storm violent enough to toss a great ship that distance, for sure no one made it to shore. I am sorry, young missy. T'were no survivors. 'Er passengers and crew alike 'ave gone to their graves on the bottom of the ocean. 'Tis a surety. May God rest their souls."

Amy knew her mouth was open, but no words came out. She tried not to cry. Tears welled in her eyes anyway and her shoulders shook.

"I knew it." Sarah burst out in sobs and buried her face in a tea towel. "I told you, Amy. I told you they were lost."

If she talked, Amy knew she would cry, too. She slipped her arm around her sister's shoulders. "I felt in my heart you were right," Amy whispered in Sarah's ear. "I hoped you were not, but deep down I realized the ship could not have been saved. Tomorrow we shall give the news to Priscilla."

Mistress Ford wiped her hands on her apron. "I have coffee," she said to the sailor. "Will you take a cup?"

He shook his head. "I must be back to my ship. There's work to be done. John waits with the skiff to ferry me out. Good day." He turned to the door, placed his cap back on his head, and in an instant had vanished into the sunny afternoon.

Amy continued to help with the washing up. She had taken over washing the dishes because Sarah was too upset. Amy's good manners superseded her sorrow and keeping busy helped hold back the tears. She confided in Mistress Ford as she soaped a trencher. "I knew all along that the ship could not survive such a storm. I shall miss my father even more now, but it is a relief to know what happened. The wonder gnawed at my insides."

"I am so sorry." Mistress Ford patted Amy's shoulder. "I too felt it had gone down but didn't want to say."

Mister William got up to help console Amy and gave her a hug. "You still 'ave your aunt and uncle," he said. "Go back to England and live with them. They'll welcome you." He went out to the forge with a sorrowful shake of his head.

Amy nodded. For right now, she continued her life as she had since she'd arrived in the colony. She taught her students, visited Priscilla to give her the news, and dreamed about the day she could sail back to her homeland.

But two nights later, while she sat eating venison stew and cornbread for supper, a loud demanding knock sounded at the door. This time a burly man with black hair and whiskers stood on the doorstep. Behind him, a skinny woman, with a dark-colored shawl wrapped around her shoulders, was partially hidden in shadow. And on the road out front, Amy saw a wagon loaded with children.

"We 'eard you have a girl 'ere who needs an 'ome," the burly man said. "We need one to work for us. We grow tobacco."

16 A Decision

"A girl?" Mister William's mouth fell open.

Mistress Ford gaped at him too. She got up from the table and wiped her hands on her apron.

"C-c-come in, p-p-please. Warm yourselves by the fire," she said, stammering out the words and wiping her hands again. "We must talk."

"Can't stay long." The woman stepped inside first. "We have eight young ones out in the wagon." She looked out the door.

The man followed. "'Tis my family," he said. "All of those youngsters are boys and my wife needs 'elp in the kitchen. 'Twould be a good 'ome. We 'ave a farm back yonder."

He gestured to the north. "Back in the trees a ways."

Amy sighed with relief. She didn't realize she had been holding her breath. At least he didn't want girls to pick worms. But she knew you didn't have to get any distance from the colony before you were alone in the forest. Would she like that? It might be as isolated as the journey through the swamp had been. And she would have to take Sarah with her.

"There's plenty for a girl to eat," the woman went on. She smiled at Amy. "Is this the one?"

"Yes," Mistress Ford said. "This is Amy. And this is her sister, Sarah."

"Oh, we only 'ave room for one girl," said the man. He looked at Sarah. "This other child is a bit young. The girl we 'ad before up and got married on us. 'Tis why we need one."

"She married a fellow she met when she came to town to do the marketing. If you get your things," the woman said to Amy, "you can come with us right now."

Things? Amy didn't have any things. Besides the gown, the apron, and the cap, all of which she was wearing, she had only the shawl Mistress Ford had knit.

"The next housemaid we get will not be leaving the cabin," the man said with a booming laugh. "Never. We'll do our own marketing. Not going to take that chance again. She'll stay in the cabin where she won't meet any people to carry 'er off."

Not leave the cabin! Go without Sarah! Never see Priscilla again! A prisoner! *My life has ended*, Amy thought.

Sarah looked back and forth between the visitors and Amy, not saying a word.

Then Mister William spoke up. "You 'ad better sit down. We need to talk." He looked at Mistress Ford and she looked back.

"Oh, we can't stay," the woman said again, "the youngsters."

I can't go away and leave my students, thought Amy. *How can I leave when I have a job to do? I can't teach anyone to read if I live off in the woods.* She knew the girls would be unable to come through the forest to lessons. Bears lived there and other animals with sharp teeth. Her students would quit. She wouldn't make any more money for her voyage. Although Sarah often annoyed her, she was the only family Amy had in this New Land. And how could she watch for Virginia? Her heart sank to her toes.

Mistress Ford wiped her hands on her apron and looked again at Mister William. "We 'ave gotten used to 'aving Amy 'ere," she said. "She 'elps me a lot. There are many 'eavy things I can no longer do. Amy does 'em for me. I'm getting old. I need her. She 'as a job with us."

"Right." Mister William stuck his sliver of wood back between his teeth. "Amy is a big 'elp. We need 'er."

"And the school!" said Charles. "We did all that work to build the schoolhouse for her."

"That's right." Mister William looked at Mistress Ford again. "Amy gives lessons in reading to girls." He beamed, as if he were talking of his own daughter. "And she is saving money to go back to England. She would be unable to stay with you long."

"Does this mean I have a job here?" Amy asked, to make sure. "While I earn enough for our trip?" She felt as if something heavy had been removed from the top of her head. She and Sarah could stay together, and close to Priscilla, too.

"You do," Mister William said with a smile.

Amy and Sarah both broke out in happy grins. "Good," Amy said. "I like it here. This is the best job I could get." The skinny woman's shoulders sagged and her smile faded.

Mistress Ford must have seen the look, too. "We shall keep an eye on ships that come in," she said. "Often an orphan who needs an 'ome is on a ship. We'll watch for you."

The man reached for the door. "We'll keep looking. Someone will come along."

* * * * *

The closer it got to the end of December, the colder the weather became. It snowed twice, too, although each time it had melted by evening meal. Amy sent her students home for a Christmas holiday and now she had her whole day to help Mistress Ford make treats.

They baked cherry tarts and apple pies. Mistress Ford made a Christmas cake and a plum pudding, both with little pieces of candied fruit that had come over on a ship from England. Amy made biscuits with honey and maple syrup for sweetener.

"I'm glad Mister Moody tells me any time he gets something special like that candied fruit in at his store." Amy rolled out another sheet of dough for sweet biscuits.

Mistress Ford dropped crushed nuts into the cake batter. "'E likes you. You teach 'is daughter."

Amy cut out biscuits shaped like stars and bells. Then she drew a pattern on a piece of paper to make special gingerbread people for everybody. She drew a huge one, more than eight inches from the top of his head to his toes. She put the pattern on the dough she had rolled out and cut around it with a sharp knife.

She made a man for everybody, one for Mistress Ford, one for Mister William, one for Sarah, one for Priscilla, one for Mistress Charity, and one for herself. Oh yes, and one for Charles, too. And she made an extra one in case they had a guest. Her mother had taught her to do that with everything.

She decorated the extra one with frosting left from the bells and stars.

After she'd finished, she hid the gingerbread men in a secret part of the cupboard behind the sacks of flour so nobody could get at them before Christmas.

I love baking, Amy thought. *And I like living in the Fords' house.* She could tell Sarah was happier, too. Sarah smiled now. And she couldn't have her thumb in her mouth when her hands were busy knitting.

"Do you know what would make Christmas day perfect?" Amy said to Sarah while she worked.

Sarah looked up from her knitting but didn't stop. She shook her head.

"If Virginia came. All those other Indians come to trade. Why doesn't he? I want to tell him how everything has turned out."

Sarah stopped knitting. "I'd like that, too. We haven't seen him since he left us on the shore."

"I want to invite him for Christmas dinner," said Amy. "Perhaps he has never had a Christmas biscuit or a slice of fruitcake."

"We don't even know where he lives. If we did, I could knit him a scarf and take it to him."

Amy nodded. "Every time a canoe full of Indians comes to town, I go down to the beach to see if Virginia is in it, but he never is. I wish he'd come."

The next day another canoe cruised along the James River. Three Indians got out and pulled it up on the sand. Amy ran to see if Virginia was with them. The visiting Indians wanted to trade dried meat and things they'd made, bows and arrows and spears, with the people. They had furs, too, from all sorts of animals. Charles got a fur with a striped tail from the animal Virginia called a raccoon. He traded a knife he'd made in the forge.

"I shall make a cap," Charles said. He plopped the fur on his head and grinned.

Not one of the Indians was Virginia. Amy went home disappointed.

She didn't have time to think much about him, however. She had to put him in the back of her mind. Everybody now kept busy preparing the house for Christmas.

Charles took the ax, and Amy went with him to the forest to cut holly. "You're not using the ax," Charles told her when she reached for it to cut a pine bough.

"I did all sorts of things that were lots harder than cutting branches while paddling up here," Amy said.

He laughed. "You keep saying that. It's a lie."

Amy left it at that. He'd never take her seriously no matter what she said. She may as well be talking to the pine tree in front of her. She grabbed the ax away from Charles and cut branches from the tree to make the house smell nice. The smoke still made her choke. Cutting the branches took her mind off Charles.

An enormous holly bush covered with bright red berries grew hidden behind the tree. She and Charles cut pieces from that, too, to decorate the rafters. They hauled everything back to the house.

The day before Christmas, when it got to be time to think about a feast, Sarah spoke up. "Can we cook Rascal for Christmas? He's the turkey I wouldn't miss."

"Good idea," Mistress Ford said. "Go out there, Charles, and get 'im. Take the ax."

Sarah and Amy hung over the chicken yard fence to watch. Rascal ran around but didn't try to attack Charles the way he did Sarah. With Charles, he ran away. Charles chased after him. "Why don't I get one of these others?" he said, panting, and sounding irritated. "They'd be easy to catch."

"No!" Sarah yelled. "It must be Rascal."

Charles took off after the runaway turkey. Once more Rascal dodged him.

"Get in the chicken yard, Sarah." Amy gave her sister a shove. "You know Rascal will attack you. He hates you."

Sarah opened the gate and took a step inside. Amy was right. Rascal snapped at Sarah's ankles with his sharp beak and flapped his wings as he ran around her.

"Don't run," Amy yelled to Sarah. "Let him come up to you. Charles can catch him."

Sarah closed her eyes and did as Amy said. She looked like she was holding her breath, too. Rascal lunged at Sarah, gobbling and mad as a hornet. Then, as if surprised because this time she didn't scream and run away, he stopped.

Charles reached out and caught him by the neck. With one swift swing of the ax, Rascal didn't have a head anymore. He staggered in a circle, blood spurting from the end of his neck, and collapsed in a heap of feathers.

Amy and Sarah both shrieked and put their hands in front of their eyes.

Charles looked at them and laughed as he hung Rascal by his feet from the chicken coop. Amy peeked out between her fingers and, after the bleeding got down to a trickle, helped pluck feathers. Charles, Amy, and Sarah all picked away until Rascal was nothing but bare skin.

The turkey kept Amy busy, and for once she forgot to check the beach for canoes.

Christmas

"No," Mistress Ford said when Amy asked if she could check the shore next day. "Christmas is for worship." She served the foods that had been prepared in advance: biscuits, sweet potato pie, a spiced ham. "I don't want to cook till sundown on the Holy Day," she explained. The turkey still hung in the larder waiting to be roasted the day after Christmas.

Amy read the Christmas story from the Bible out loud for everyone, and when bells rang out at noon, she walked to church services with Mister and Mistress Ford, Sarah, and Charles. The deacon read the Christmas story again, and the priest himself led prayers.

When at last they left church, Amy still was not allowed to check the beach, but she saw a canoe out on the water. "Perhaps it's coming here," she whispered to Sarah, nudging her.

Sarah smiled and nodded.

When the sun disappeared, Amy chopped onions and bread to make a stuffing for the turkey and get it ready for roasting the next day. She knew better than to ask again if she could check the shore. With preparations for tomorrow's festivities completed, she curled up in front of the fire in her quilts.

Next morning, the weak December sun forced its way through the small cabin window and woke Amy. "Sarah," she said, shaking her sister's arm. "Let's check. Hurry. If that canoe was Virginia's, we don't want to miss him."

As fast as she could, Amy dressed in her best things: the petticoat Priscilla had made and the new stockings Mistress Ford had knit. She put on her apron, her tea towel cap, and her new shoes with brass buckles that she had finally been able to buy. Now she looked like a proper English girl instead of a wild one.

"Virginia won't know me if he is here," Amy said with a laugh. Hand in hand she and Sarah ran to the beach. The chill December air turned their breath frosty and the frozen mud crunched beneath their shoes.

"Look! That dugout did come here!" Sarah exclaimed.

Please let it be Virginia, Amy said over and over to herself as she raced along. A lone Indian huddled next to a small fire beside the lapping waves.

"I think it's him," Sarah said. "I really and truly do."

"Virginia!" Amy called. "Is it you?"

The Indian turned to face her. It was Virginia all right. Amy hadn't seen him in weeks, but he hadn't changed. His hair still stuck up in that familiar ridge, and he had those same feathers and shells poked into it. He wore a long-sleeved deerskin shirt now and leggings, also deerskin slippers on his feet. He stood with a wide, wide smile, his teeth gleaming white in his brown face.

Amy ran to him and threw her arms around his neck. "Oh, I've checked the shore so many times for you. I'm delighted you've come to visit."

Sarah flung herself on Virginia as well. "I thought you'd never call on us," she said.

Virginia hugged back. "Hello," he said, beaming. "Hello, Amy. Hello, Sarah."

Amy didn't let go of his hand. Now that he was here, she wasn't going to. "We're having a feast today," she said. "Eat. Supper. You must come."

She wanted to show him off to Mister and Mistress Ford. It didn't matter if other people didn't invite Indians to their homes; she did. She tugged on his arm. "Come on. Throw sand on the fire, Sarah, and bring the spears and arrows. Virginia wouldn't want to go anywhere without those."

After smothering the fire, Sarah picked up his weapons and followed her sister along the shore.

He looked at what she'd done and smiled. "T'ank you, Sarah."

As the girls and Virginia walked back to the Fords' house, Amy saw people peeking from behind curtains. She ignored them.

Virginia hesitated at the doorway, as if he didn't want to go all the way in. He put his hand on the door frame, and held himself back.

"Come on," Amy coaxed, pulling on his arm.

"Go in," Sarah said. She pushed at his back. "It's warm."

Amy guessed he'd never before been inside an English house.

Mister William put his hand up like everyone did when they met an Indian. "Welcome," Mister William said. "Come in. Have coffee with cream."

Virginia must have thought it was all right if Mister William invited him. He stepped into the house and walked toward the fireplace. He smiled. "Fire," he said. "Good."

Sarah came in last and closed the door. She propped Virginia's spears against the wall and gave Mistress Ford and Mister William a wide, wide smile. "This is Virginia," Sarah said. "He's our friend."

Mistress Ford opened her eyes wide with amazement but brought up a stool so Virginia could sit by the fire. Amy knew he would prefer the floor. "I'll make coffee," Mistress Ford said. "Anyone 'oo is a friend of Amy's and Sarah's is welcome 'ere. We are grateful to you for 'elping and caring for 'em."

Amy knew Virginia didn't understand what Mistress Ford said, but when everybody else smiled, so did he. He sat on the floor, ignoring the stool.

Charles sat at the table with a bowl of oatmeal in front of him, not eating. His raised spoon dripped cereal on Mistress Ford's special tablecloth with the embroidered holly. His mouth gaped open.

Amy noticed and grinned. "This is Virginia," she said. "He's my best friend."

Charles closed his mouth and swallowed. "Uh...p...p...pleased to meet you," he stammered, looking confused.

While Sarah turned the spit in the fireplace to roast the turkey evenly, Amy showed Virginia things that were different from what they had used when the four of them traveled together. She brought out books, the checkers game, the shawls, quilts folded and stored in the chest in the corner. And she took him outside to look at the schoolhouse.

Back inside, Mistress Ford served coffee in the silver cups Amy had seen stored on the top shelf of the cupboard. "They came from England," Mistress Ford said. "I use them on special days." Virginia picked one up, careful not to spill any coffee. He rubbed a finger over the engraving and looked at Amy, puzzled.

"Cup," Amy said. "Like a gourd." She took a sip from her own.

"Cup," Virginia said and made a face when he tasted the coffee.

Amy put honey in it, a drop or two of thick cream, and stirred it with one of the special silver spoons that went with the cups.

He took another sip. "Ah," he said.

"Better?" Amy asked.

"Better," Virginia repeated. "*Winganouse.*"

"That means good," said Amy.

"You speak Indian language?" Charles asked.

"A word or two," said Amy.

Charles watched Virginia the whole time they drank. After they'd had the coffee, he asked, "Do you know how to play checkers?"

"He knows some English words, but he wouldn't understand that," Sarah said.

"It's a game," Amy explained. "Play. Game."

Virginia still looked mystified, but sat ready to try.

"I'll show you." Amy set the checkers up on the board. She and Charles started to play.

She picked up a red checker. "I'm red," she said. She picked up a black one. "Charles is black."

Virginia caught on fast. For someone who couldn't understand the English words and learned by what he saw, instead of by what he was told, he caught on extra quick.

By the time Mistress Ford had dinner on the table, he'd beaten Charles four times. Charles didn't look like he believed it. "You mean you traveled all the way through the swamp with this savage?" he asked. "You girls and him?"

Amy and Sarah both nodded.

"Did you teach him the English words?"

They nodded a second time.

"He can make a fire without a flint," Sarah said with pride.

"I didn't know you could do what the savages do. I could never do that." A small smile crept onto Charles's face.

Amy snorted. "So now you think I'm clever?"

Mister William shook his head. "This man is not a savage. 'E is to be admired. 'E cared for and protected these girls during a difficult journey. 'E didn't 'ave to do that. 'E did it because 'e is a good person. I guess all Indians aren't savages."

Charles nodded.

Amy smiled as Mister Ford's acceptance of Virginia radiated throughout the room. She felt warm inside and out.

Priscilla and Mistress Charity arrived to eat Christmas dinner with them. "We have a surprise," Amy said, as she flung the door wide.

"Look who's here!" said Sarah, jumping up from the floor.

Priscilla flung her hands in front of her face then beamed from ear to ear and wrapped her arms around Virginia's neck like Amy and Sarah had done. "What a wonderful s'prise," she said. "Now Christmas is perfect."

Virginia did sit on a bench, Amy on one side of him and Priscilla the other, while he ate dinner. He picked up a fork and studied it.

"It's a fork," Amy said, "to eat with." She speared a carrot with her own and put it in her mouth.

"We 'aven't 'ad the blessing," Mistress Ford scolded.

Amy put her fork down and bowed her head while Mister William spoke the words.

Virginia watched in wonder. Then he picked up his own fork and did what Amy had done. He grinned. "Fork," he said. "Eat. Fork." He used it for a lot of the dinner, but when a piece of sweet potato fell off, he gave up and ate with his hands. He didn't bother to cut the meat, but picked up a whole turkey leg and chewed on it that way. Nobody criticized. Mistress Ford handed him two large tea towels to wipe his hands.

After dinner, Amy noticed Mister William go out to the forge. He returned smiling and carrying something big. "New game," he said, putting it on the table.

Everyone came to look, all except Sarah who still scrubbed away on the gravy pan. "What is it?" Amy asked.

"It's chess," Charles said. "I helped make it out of little bits of scrap iron from the forge. The knights were the most difficult." Half of the pieces had been painted white, half left regular iron color.

"I don't know how to play," Amy said. "You'll have to show me, Mister William."

"I'll do it," said Charles. "I know. I played with my brothers in England. I have six brothers. Amy will learn fast."

Amy wondered what had changed his mind about her. Perhaps because she had an Indian friend. Or maybe now he had to believe she'd traveled through the swamp, since Virginia confirmed it.

"Maybe I'll let you teach me to read sometime. What I said before was not true." Charles smiled and turned ruby red beneath his freckles.

Priscilla hid a giggle with her hand and Amy raised both eyebrows at this statement, but neither said anything about it. "Right now I have a surprise, too," Amy said and went to the secret place where she'd hidden the gingerbread men. She passed one to each person: Mister William, Mistress Ford, Charles, Priscilla, and Mistress Charity. She put one on the table for Sarah if she ever got done scrubbing, and handed the special one, the one with the extra maple flavored frosting, to Virginia. "Sweet biscuit," Amy explained to Virginia. "You eat it." She took a bite of her own, the gingerbread man's whole head.

Virginia bit a foot off his. He smiled. "Good biscuit."

Everyone took a bite of their gingerbread man, even Sarah, who had finished her scrubbing at long last.

"I 'ave 'ot apple cider," Mistress Ford said. She headed for the pot hanging from its hook in the fireplace. "'Tis spiced."

Sarah groaned. "Oh, no, more things to wash." But she smiled.

"I shall clean up next time," Mistress Ford offered. "You girls 'ave been doing my work for weeks. 'Tis my turn now. I don't want to forget 'ow." She laughed.

"Will you come to visit us again?" Sarah asked Virginia, accepting her cup of cider from Mistress Ford. "Visit," she repeated. She swept her arm around to indicate the hearth.

"Will you?" Amy asked. "Come here. Visit." She patted the floor.

"Here," Virginia copied. "Visit. Here." He smiled and patted the floor like Amy had.

"Come tomorrow," said Sarah.

"Does he understand?" Mistress Ford asked.

"He does," said Amy. "He's clever." She felt warm all over, and it wasn't the hot cider. It was spending cozy time with people who cared for each other. "This is the best day I've had since that storm started to blow," she said. And she thought, *I can't go back to England and give this up. Virginia would never be able to visit me over there. I'd never see him again. I couldn't stand that. I've lost Father. I don't want to lose Virginia.*

Would Mister William let her and Sarah stay? That first day they had been in the Fords' home, he'd said he didn't want girls around. Would he want them now? If she didn't return to her homeland, would she have to be a prisoner with someone like that tobacco farmer? Or the man who wanted a housekeeper?

"Couldn't we stay here with you?" Amy asked Mister William.

"Of course you may." He was emphatic and slipped his arm around Amy's shoulders. "Stay 'ere. I always thought you wanted to go back to your aunt and uncle."

Sarah sat with a grin that almost met her ears and clapped her hands.

Mistress Ford smiled, too. "I've liked 'aving you girls 'ere," she said. "You're a big 'elp and good company, Amy—and Sarah, too. I thought you had your 'eart set on returning to England, or I would 'ave said so sooner."

Mister William got up and knocked his pipe out in the fireplace. He refilled it. "This is your 'ome as long as you need it. Forever if that be the case. You know, I shall like 'aving girls around." He smiled.

Priscilla reached for Amy's hand. "Yes stay," she said. "I 'ave always wanted you to."

"You're family now," Mistress Ford said. "Call me 'Attie, as William does."

"And please, call me William. With no mister. I 'ate stuffy titles." He laughed and took a stick from the fire to relight the pipe.

Amy smiled back. She felt wanted. "This is my home. I like it here. I like my new friends. I have learned to do many things I never thought I'd be able to manage before." She smiled at Hattie, and William, and Virginia, and Priscilla. She smiled at Charles, too.

She didn't feel lost any more. She didn't feel alone when all these good folks surrounded her. "Now I am glad I didn't go back to England to live," Amy said. "It's sad to think I will never see my homeland again, but I shall stay here with all of you good friends. I'll write to Edmund tomorrow. This colony is my home now."

She sat on the hearth with her cup of cider and leaned against Virginia's back, each of them holding the other one up, the same as they had on their journey.

Educational Resources

Glossary

Croatoan. An Indian tribe of North Carolina.

crosstrees. Two short bars across a ship's mast that support the sails.

forge. A place where metal is heated and hammered into shape.

gentry. People of high social standing; just below nobility.

hold. The part of a ship below the lowest deck where cargo is stored.

horn book. A sheet of parchment with letters on it mounted on a board and protected by a thin layer of horn from a cow.

indenture. An agreement stating someone is to work for another for a given length of time.

ketch. A sailboat with two masts.

lee side. The sheltered side of a ship away from the wind.

oyster. A sea animal with an irregular shell; similar to a clam.

petticoat. An underskirt worn under a dress.

shift. A shapeless garment worn next to the skin beneath a dress and petticoat. This was the only underwear worn by girls in the seventeenth century.

skiff. A small, light rowboat.

slate. A thin sheet of dark-colored rock for writing on with chalk.

tallow. Colorless, tasteless fat from cattle, sheep, etc., used in making candles.

tinder. Dry, easily flammable material for starting a fire.

topside. The upper or main deck of a ship.

trencher. A wooden board used as a plate.

'tween deck. The area between the main deck and hold of a ship.

venison. Meat from a deer.

Indian words

assimoest. Fox.

messetts. Feet.

nammais. Fish.

nekut. One.

netab. Friend.

ninge. Two.

winganouse. Very good.

Study Topics and Questions

1. What else could Amy, Priscilla, and Sarah have done to survive on the beach?

2. Could they eat seaweed?

3. Could they fashion a fishnet from their clothes? If they did, and they were successful, how could they cook what they caught?

4. Should they sit there and just keep their fingers crossed for another storm so they would get more drinking water?

5. Maybe another ship would be wrecked. What if it were a pirate ship? Or the dreaded Spanish? What might happen to them then?

6. Why were they afraid of the Spanish?

7. Was going with Virginia the best decision?

8. What would you have done?

9. What animals could they have met during their trip through the Great Dismal Swamp?

10. How about trees? What kinds of trees grow in a swamp?

11. Jamestown was the first permanent English settlement in what is now America. What was second? Can you think of something significant about that second settlement?

12. In *On Their Own* we got a pretty good description of the clothes girls wore in 1627. What did boys wear?

13. How did the colonists know which plants they could eat?

14. The fictitious character Virginia, whom you met in this novel, was not the only historic person to be named Virginia. Who was Virginia Dare?

15. Virginia took the girls to the "Ghost Colony." This is actually a famous failed colony in North Carolina. Look up Roanoke Island and the Lost Colony either on the Internet or in an encyclopedia and see what you find.

16. Why did the Jamestown colony succeed when Roanoke failed?

Activities

Construct a diorama of a colonial village. Use the Internet and an encyclopedia to find pictures. Colonial buildings were roofed with thatch. Tie dead grass into bundles for the pretend thatch.

Research

Do a report on the tobacco industry:

◆ Which states now grow tobacco?

◆ Which one grows the most? Show this using a bar graph.

◆ What are some of the effects of smoking tobacco?

◆ Nicotine is a chemical found in tobacco. Are there good uses for nicotine?

Science

Make a chart for this month's moon phases. You can find them in an almanac or on some calendars. How does *On Their Own* use the phases of the moon to show the passage of time? How long is a complete moon cycle?

Additional Educational Resources

Visit these websites for additional information and activities.
>
> http://www.historyisfun.org/
> http://www.historyglobe.com/jamestown/

Selected Bibliography

The Native Americans: The Indigenous People of North America. Salamander Books Ltd., 1991.

The World of the American Indian. National Geographic Society, 1974.

World Book Encyclopedia.

www.wicocomico-indian-nation.com/pages/dictionary.html